Donald MacKenzie and The Murder Room

》》》 This title is part of The Murder Room, our series dedicated to making available out-of-print or hard-to-find titles by classic crime writers.

Crime fiction has always held up a mirror to society. The Victorians were fascinated by sensational murder and the emerging science of detection; now we are obsessed with the forensic detail of violent death. And no other genre has so captivated and enthralled readers.

Vast troves of classic crime writing have for a long time been unavailable to all but the most dedicated frequenters of second-hand bookshops. The advent of digital publishing means that we are now able to bring you the backlists of a huge range of titles by classic and contemporary crime writers, some of which have been out of print for decades.

From the genteel amateur private eyes of the Golden Age and the femmes fatales of pulp fiction, to the morally ambiguous hard-boiled detectives of mid twentieth-century America and their descendants who walk our twenty-first century streets, The Murder Room has it all. 》》》

The Murder Room
Where Criminal Minds Meet

themurderroom.com

Donald MacKenzie 1908–1994

Donald MacKenzie was born in Ontario, Canada, and educated in England, Canada and Switzerland. For twenty-five years MacKenzie lived by crime in many countries. 'I went to jail,' he wrote, 'if not with depressing regularity, too often for my liking.' His last sentences were five years in the United States and three years in England, running consecutively. He began writing and selling stories when in American jail. 'I try to do exactly as I like as often as possible and I don't think I'm either psychopathic, a wayward boy, a problem of our time, a charming rogue. Or ever was.'

He had a wife, Estrela, and a daughter, and they divided their time between England, Portugal, Spain and Austria.

Scent of Danger

Donald MacKenzie

An Orion book

Copyright © The Estate of Donald MacKenzie 1958

The right of Donald MacKenzie to be identified as the author of this work has been asserted in accordance with the Copyright, Designs and Patents Act 1988.

This edition published by
The Orion Publishing Group Ltd
Orion House
5 Upper St Martin's Lane
London WC2H 9EA

An Hachette UK company
A CIP catalogue record for this book is available from the British Library

ISBN 978 1 4719 0563 6

www.orionbooks.co.uk

For John and Judy Cuninghame

SATURDAY

THE TWO men sat in the great house, waiting. In the faint light of summer dawn, the child's head was dark against the cot pillow. Through the open door to the nursery, the governess slept heavily.

With the sound of the stopping car, both men moved to the corridor. Across twelve feet of board and carpet, they could see into the bedroom. At the side of the fourposter bed a shaded light burned. A white silk coverlet had been turned back. On the small table, a water carafe and tumbler flanked a bottle of sleeping-tablets.

As the street door closed, the older man gestured, his right sleeve flapping where arm became stump at the wrist. Bain pushed his shoulders hard into the wall behind him. Both men were still as the stairs creaked gently under the weight of mounting feet.

Bain could still see the corridor. She stood, the woman, in the square of her own doorway. When she yawned, the light caught the blaze of diamond from head, throat and arm. For a moment, she turned her head towards the nursery door then yawned again and went into the bedroom. The lock clicked with finality as she turned the key from the inside.

Already, Bain's fingers had found the barrel-nosed forceps in his pocket. He felt the smooth metal gratefully, content that the waiting was almost over. Three hours they'd been in this house—seven sleeping bodies around them. The last uneasy half hour in the child's nursery. Once, the child had moved in sleep, tossing the covers. Arran replaced them, crossing the room without sound—in the darkness almost without substance.

Bain knew the way his partner reasoned. Without motive other than self-preservation. A cold child woke more readily

1

than a warm one. It was no more than that. Arran's acceptance of his position as a lawbreaker was complete. Since
the commission of crime endangered him, every act must
be designed for self-protection. Chance was an enemy,
never a friend. Bain had worked with twenty guys but
never a better one than Arran.

The strip of light at the bottom of the door disappeared.
The two men waited ten more minutes then tiptoed quietly
into the corridor, closing the nursery door behind them.
Need for action had rid Bain's stomach of the knot of fear
and his gloved hands worked surely. Gentle fingers found
the nose of the key and fitted it into the jaws of the forceps.
Exerting pressure with both hands, he turned the forceps
against the clock until the wards clicked. Completing the
circle, he stood back, wetting his mouth. As always, sweat
had started to drench the back of his shirt.

The half-empty sleeve flapped and Bain rotated the door
handle, pushing gently. The white door ajar, they waited
in the warm air, heavy with a scent no longer fresh. The
velvet curtains were drawn and the room dark. With conscious deference, he waited for Arran to give the signal.
Though each had given equally in the preparation, it was
the older man's coup. An assault planned with more than
intelligence—with a cold hostility that Arran found for
each individual he robbed. Both men had spent long restless
hours in the pursuit of servants. Days in the Reference
Rooms of public libraries, searching the history of the
Middleburgh family. Turning up old files of *Country Life*
till the right copy was found. Four illustrated pages with
photographs and plan of the interior of Middleburgh
House. Arran's imagination had given probability to a
scheme that other screwsmen would have laughed off.
Maybe it *was* true that the heirlooms came out of the bank
three or four times a year, he argued, maybe the Duchess
was burglar-conscious. But at four in the morning, people
become careless. All that was left was to watch the social
columns. And the Duchess.

They'd seen her off from the house on Belgrave Square. Walked past her car where it waited in line in front of the Palace. Watched as she chatted with the girl she was to present. Waited till she came home, a tired woman.

Now, at the end of it all, Bain was even more ready to accept Arran's leadership. He scarcely believed in the reward any more. Those jewels that had flashed in the light might be paste. Only danger was real and he needed Arran to lead him out of it.

In the immense bed, the woman showed in the tiny circle of light from the pencil flash Arran held in his teeth. Mouth half open, she trailed a hand in drugged sleep. Moving with sure economy, each man took up position. Arran, at the dressing-table, held a black velvet bag in his good hand. The stump he used, with awful dexterity, to scoop the jewellery into the bag. By the bed, Bain sneaked a look at his partner. His own job was to watch the open door—the woman on the bed. The flat weight of the gun in his pocket was an assurance. The first faint creak of the trigger brought a feeling of power. With it, no desire to destroy but the satisfaction of imposing one's will. In the disc of light at the dressing-table, hand and stump worked faster, rejecting trinkets, choosing only gem stones. Bain pulled his eyes back to the woman. She had not moved. He looked at Arran who jerked the flash in his mouth at the door. Then the room went dark. Closing the door on the sleeping woman, Bain followed his partner to the head of the stairs.

Down below, light filtered into the wide hall. The two men worked quickly, a nod, a gesture, sufficient communication. The two mortise locks on the door were fastened—the keys gone—he used the skeleton keys. The short length of burglar chain clinked softly as he undid it. For a second, he waited for the creak of a servant's door to open. But the house still slept. Gently, he lowered the chain and pulled back the catch of the spring lock. The heavy street door opened easily on oiled hinges.

Beyond the tall iron railings that enclosed the wet green

in the centre of the square, an early sun filtered through the plane trees. From far off, the sounds came as they might in the country. Clear and with the faintest echo. A dog barking—bottle cages clanging in a milk cart.

Bain checked his watch. Thirty seconds to wait. With the sound of the first, heavy footsteps in the square, he narrowed the slit in the door. The uniformed police walked slowly in file, swinging capes no longer necessary in the morning warmth. A dozen or so men whose night beat covered the area. In a couple of minutes, they would check in at Gerald Road Police Station to be replaced with the first shift of the day. During that brief lapse in surveillance, the square was unprotected.

The two men left the house without hurry. Once again, Bain used the two skeleton keys to make fast the door. One thing remained to betray their defeat of the locks, the unfastened burglar chain on the other side of the door. From the top of the stone flight to the window sill was a long step. Bain made it, steadying himself with one hand. He crouched there. In a second, he would be through the window in front of him. There were no screws to secure the sashes. No patent catches or clanging burglar alarms to signal his entry. But set on each side of the window frame were two electronic cells. As soon as he passed through the beam, a warning would flash at Gerald Road Police Station, five hundred yards away. Within minutes, the square would be full of police. Yet a few more minutes and the radio control room at Scotland Yard would be in action—a dozen squad cars sealing off the area.

Bain slid the putty knife between the sashes, pushing back the catch. Then he eased up the window. If their luck held, if Arran's guess was good, they'd be out of the area before the cops were mobilised. What they'd come to do in that house was almost done—not about to be started. The tell-tale rays were no secret to them. Once again, it had been the dreary nights and evenings spent in the public libraries that paid off. It was in some obscure trade journal that Arran had found the advertisement.

THE GIMLET RAY—THE WATCHDOG THAT NEVER SLEEPS

In a feature article was a technical account of its installation in the houses of half a dozen celebrities. Middleburgh House was among them.

Bain steadied himself on gloved hands and looked over his shoulder. At the top of the steps, Arran was almost elegant in his portrayal of innocence. His maimed right hand was lost in his trouser pocket. Grey hair toffee-streaked with sun, his blue suit and white silk shirt still fresh, he nodded down encouragement as if to a dog to which he was giving an early morning run. Easily, Bain vaulted the sill into the dining-room. A tall dark clock in the corner whirred the quarter hour as he ran into the hall. Nothing else moved. He passed the straightbacked chairs, like silent guests against the wall, and lifted the burglar chain. Swiftly, he fastened its snout in the slot. Refastening the mortise lock, he ran back to the open window. A moment more and he was up beside Arran at the head of the steps. One last look for dirt on their clothes and both men walked across the square to the parked car. Behind them, the great house was still silent.

Bain took the ignition keys from his pocket. For three nights they'd watched this Vanguard saloon. Daytimes, a woman from one of the houses beyond used the car. In an accessory shop off the Euston Road, Bain had found the right combination of keys for door and ignition. Now he hit the starting button, then gunned the motor. Heading the car south, he drove fast into the wide empty sweep of Grosvenor Gardens.

"Three minutes. You couldn't have done it better." Arran's face was tranquil. With his good hand, he fingered the grey stubble on his cheek. "Take it a little slower," he ordered. "We're off the district and this car won't be missed for a while."

5

Without question, Bain eased the car to thirty. Arran's quiet certainty made danger impossible. Once across Vauxhall Bridge, Bain drove west along the river. Here, the day's work had already begun. Crane booms swung noisily. Tugs nosed laden barges into the shelter of the wharves. Long-distance trucks blocked the roadway, their drivers bellowing abuse at one another. On past a paper mill, the Vanguard turned on to a deserted wharf. There was no gate—no office—no more than a hundred yards of bare stone cluttered with baled waste, twenty feet high.

Bain edged the stolen car to the side of the water. The Vanguard was hidden, now, from both mill and road.

"Three-quarters of an hour before they open here," he said. It was the first time he had spoken since they had got into the car and his voice croaked with nervousness. He pulled down the window and spat at the water beneath. "Shall I dump this stuff now?" He nodded down at his new, scuffed shoes. For seven hours, the thick crêpe soles had allowed him to trip lightly. Now they hurt like hell. On the floor, in front of the back seat, were two pairs of leather-soled shoes. They had changed in the Vanguard before going into the house.

Arran's eyes were blue—bright and without depth. "Well, that's the last time you ever use a bunch of keys," he said thoughtfully. "You went out on a high note. I've seen the best of them at work. Tonight was a . . . " he waved the flapping sleeve ". . . a tour de force." In his mouth, there was no incongruousness in the expression.

Bain bent over his shoe laces, hiding his pleasure. Too often, the mockery in Arran's eyes robbed his praise of value. Bain kicked his feet free of the hot suède. In turn, Arran let his own shoes fall to the floor and flexed his toes. Bain tied two sets of shoe laces together and stuffed the putty knife in a glove. Then the strip of celluloid he had used for the spring lock. For a second, his hands lingered with the slender skeleton keys. These had been cut with laborious care from square blanks. Last of all, he threw the short automatic on the pile.

Working his fingers, Arran eased the glove from his left hand. It fell at his feet and Bain retrieved it. "What do you think you're doing with that gun—those keys?" asked Arran.

Bain looked up, forcing from his face the scowl that always accompanied a question. It was a mannerism that irritated the other. Lighting a cigarette, Bain let the match fall to the sluggish water beneath. "I'm going to dump them with the rest. There!"

Nose thin with a non-smoker's dislike, Arran opened the window on his side. "I see," he said, too pleasantly. "All the evidence in one tidy package for the police to find." He stabbed his stump towards Bain. "If some boy burglars have just dumped a safe *there*," he mocked, "the cops may well be dragging the river in an hour's time."

Bain waited, without answer. Sometimes, he toyed with the idea of erasing that quiet smile from the other's face. During the two years that they had worked together, the older man had never been wrong. Indifferent to all but their joint safety, Arran used his inner certainty like a whip. And, Christ, you grew sick of being always on the receiving end of it.

"Two skeleton keys that fit two locks at that house," Arran continued. He was leaning back, his eyes not completely closed. Suddenly he opened them wide. "And all the usual screwsman's impedimenta." Long ago, something had smacked with force into his upper lip, scarring and thickening the tissue. It gave his smile a lopsided appearance. Delicately, he took the burning stub from Bain and pitched it into the river. "No, Mac! It makes their job too simple! If the cops should drag here—if any snotty-nosed brat with a line on the end of a pole starts to fish—the catch won't be remarkable. Three gloves. Two pairs of shoes and a piece of 'loid. Nothing to connect them with Belgrave

Square." He shook his head. "But with the keys! That gun. . . ."

Already, Bain had separated pistol and keys from the pile. He kept his voice civil. "Then what?" he asked. "What do you suggest I do with them?"

One-handed, Arran was tying the knots in his shoe laces. "Do you intend to sleep now or what?"

"For two hours?" jibed Bain. "It's not worth it. I'll take a bath and collect my ticket. Sleep I can get tonight."

"Good." The pale eyes were level. "That's probably best. What time will you be ready to go out?"

Bain moved his shoulders. "Nine-thirty—ten. As long as it takes me to get a shower and change my clothing. I've got no woman to bother about." As he spoke, he regretted it. The suggestion that Arran's will could be weakened, his perfection blemished, because of his wife, would be unwelcome.

The older man was unmoved. "Caroline does as she's told," he said shortly. "Write down this address." He waited as Bain took pen and paper.

Bain scribbled street and number on the back of the envelope. Once a coup had been made—the time for action gone—he was always ill-at-ease with his partner. Taut with need to placate—to avoid the word that might trip the other's displeasure.

"Get to that address—at ten," said Arran. "Ask for Corrigan. You don't know him but he'll be expecting you. And say as little as possible to him. I don't want him remembering you, particularly. That accent of yours sticks out a mile. Just give him the keys and the gun. He'll know what to do with them."

"OK." Bain pocketed the paper. With Arran, there was no point in much questioning. You merely left yourself wide open for the inevitable feeling of inferiority.

Cigarette ash had greyed the blue of the older man's jacket and he brushed at it impatiently. "Your bit of gymnastics at the window will convince everyone," he said at last. "Including the woman upstairs. She'll sleep till the law gets there. When she wakes, she won't know whether her stuff went at four o'clock or at six. What she *will* know is that her street door will have been found locked with the burglar chain still on." He rapped a finger at the other's knee. "It's cutting it fine, but there *is* just time for a villain to have been in through that window, up to the bedroom and out again, the way he came. *You* made that possible."

The sun had climbed, giving a rippling sheen to the black water beneath. Already, the stream of city-bound buses on the bridge beyond was heavier. Bain was suddenly restless. "All right," he said. "I give this guy Corrigan the keys and the gun. When do I meet you?"

Arran ignored the question. "In two months' time, that jewellery will have been replaced. Those keys will be worth money."

"With us in Spain?" It was impossible to go *on* playing straight man to another's cleverness.

"Corrigan doesn't know where those keys may be used. In six months' time, I propose to tell him. For thirty-three and a third of the loot." Arran stretched his legs, polishing the tips of his black shoes on the carpet. "Sometimes cops are only too ready to believe in their own logic, Mac. Whoever screws that house for the second time will be assumed to have done it the first. When that happens, as you point out, we'll be in Spain."

Unable to follow completely the other's reasoning, Bain's inquiry was a plea for reassurance. "Suppose it's a tumble, the second time. How solid is this guy? How do you know he won't bawl his head off?"

Arran's lip was thick as he smiled. "Because, like you and me, Corrigan's an exceptional rogue. We all believe there are certain things required of us for self-protection. You don't steal your pal's cut. You don't involve others in your trouble with the police." He bent, making a package of shoes and gloves. Reaching past Bain, he let the bundle fall. It hit the water and a few gulls circled curiously as the leather soaked. When it sank, they flapped off. "All we give Corrigan is reliable information, in six months' time. If he doesn't know that the place was burgled last night, it's his headache. Crime reports are required reading for thieves. Corrigan can take care of himself, Mac. Let me do the same for us."

Eager now to be in the safety of Arran's car, parked a quarter mile away, Bain nodded. "And when do we meet?" he asked again.

"At noon at the airport. Once you see me and Caroline there, forget about us until we get to Madrid." Reaching in his pocket, Arran spilled the contents of the bag on his lap. Against the dark blue stuff, the diamonds flashed light from a hundred facets. This was no modern jewellery, cut to deceive, but gems without time in fashion. Five carat stones studded each point of the ducal tiara. The bracelets, made when St Petersburg had a court jeweller, showed beauty beyond the double row of brilliants. His face expressionless, Arran considered the jewels in his lap. Then he put them away.

He spoke with satisfaction. "In an hour's time, Rojas will have broken this stuff up. I told you at the beginning that this coup would pay us." He turned to Bain, his face smiling fully for the first time. "You know what we're going to cut up! Forty thousand dollars. Nearly eight thousand pounds apiece. And you'll take your end, the way you like it, in Madrid. In any currency in the world." His voice was amused. "By the way, have you got enough money for your hotel bill—the plane ticket?"

From beginning to end, everything had been as Arran had promised it would be. His quiet menace—the certainty that verged on smugness—were directed at those who stood in his way. Not at those who were with him. Bain thought of the few pounds in his pocket and now amusement showed on his face. "Sure—I've got enough," he said.

The two men checked the smooth surfaces of the Vanguard with care. Since their gloves had been removed, here and there their fingers had rested, no matter how briefly. Each used a handkerchief, polishing until no possibility of a print remained. It was half past eight as they walked off the wharf.

For six months, Bain had lived at the hotel at the back of Knightsbridge. A small place, with no more than twenty rooms. He was accepted there without question as a Canadian journalist. A pose that covered his unconventional comings and goings.

At the corner of the Crescent, Arran braked to a stop, using his maimed right arm with the efficiency that always troubled Bain. That, the multiple scars that covered Arran's body, implied a physical menace. The man's quiet voice and manner only added to it. Arran was a sun-worshipper. A hundred times, over these past two years, Bain had watched his partner move around, stripped to the shorts. The red-brown skin on chest and back livid with scar tissue. As though the flesh had been whipped with a cat o' nine tails. More from fear than courtesy, Bain had bitten down on his curiosity. Once, his face to the sun, polishing his scarred skin with his left hand, Arran's eyes had opened with a suddenness that caught Bain unaware.

"A great healer, the sun." It was the nearest that Arran had ever got to an explanation.

Groups of women were hurrying past the parked car on their way to the big department store on the corner. In a quarter hour, the store would be open. Three hours more and passengers for the Madrid plane would be moving into their channel. Gun and keys were flat in his hip pocket. Bain opened the door.

"The airport, then, at twelve."

Arran nodded. "Twelve." He started the motor. "Corrigan'll be expecting you, so be on time. *Ciau!*" he said and waved his right arm.

Bain walked over to the hotel entrance without looking back. It was a family concern where the owners worked hard, late and early. Already, Emil was behind the small reception desk, sorting mail. As Bain took his key, the Swiss smiled. It was a greeting reserved for new guests and those who paid their bills promptly. He riffled through the stacked letters.

"Nothing for you today, Mr Bain. But I have your account ready. My wife tells me you are leaving this morning." The cash drawer was open and the man's fingers hovered over the notes and silver. As though reluctant to part with any, even in change. "You will be long out of England, Mr Bain?"

He made no answer. With luck, for ever. Just hours now and this city would be a memory of three trials, three convictions. A half dozen years spent in stinking jails. It needed only one more conviction and some po-faced bastard in a wig would be sentencing him as an habitual criminal. To twelve years—ten—eight. It didn't matter. The least of them was a death sentence. Even at thirty-five, better a rope to the bars and your neck than a grey succession of days without hope.

He shoved three five-pound notes across the counter and checked the thin wad that remained. Forty quid. The plane ticket would cost twenty. Ah well. He'd neither drink nor eat another twenty before the plane reached Madrid.

Emil stamped and receipted the bill. The lines round his mouth were deep with pleasure. "And two make fifteen! Thank you, sir. Just a card to let us know when you'll be coming back and your room will be ready." He closed the drawer sharply and pocketed the key. His interest in Bain was over.

Upstairs, the room was as Bain had left it. The bed turned back and unused. The cabin trunk, locked and strapped, consigned to storage. If he never saw the trunk again, it wouldn't matter. It held clothes. A few souvenirs from the RCN. A couple of photographs of his parents, the set kindly smiles on their faces a mockery of that last letter. It had been his mother who had written. The words were too few and final to forget.

'If I thought you would care, Macbeth, I would tell you of the shame and hurt that you have caused your father and me. We grieved for a son and no longer have one.'

That was five years ago. Now the letter and photographs had become part of his self-justification. Reminders that you never went back. For there was nothing to go back to. The hell with it. Like everything else in that trunk, the souvenirs could rot. Eight thousand pounds was more than just money. It was goodbye to a life full of fear.

He walked past the trunk to the bathroom. Stripped, he took the cold needles of the shower with gratitude, rubbing the sleep from eyes and temples. Once he had shaved, he felt alive again. The grey mohair suit was still good. He dressed with care, knotting the blue knitted tie neatly. Yesterday's carnation was unwilted in a tooth-mug. Wearing a *boutonnière* to a burglary was an affectation that had not survived Arran's sarcasm. But Bain still wore a flower and as if the gesture marked the end of an era, he set it in his lapel.

It was five past nine. He checked his pockets. Cash, Corrigan's address. The gun and keys would be bulky in the thin tropical suit. He wrapped them in newspaper and stuffed the package into a briefcase together with passport and ticket voucher. He took one last look at the room. The storage people would collect the trunk later. His bags he could pick up on the way to the airport. Indifferent to the elevator, he took the steps down, two at a time.

On the street, he flagged a passing cab. At Hyde Park Corner, they drew abreast of a local radio car. The cop at the wheel had his uniform cap tipped back. Sweating, he wiped his forehead. Bain grinned. Arran was right. The sun was a great transformer. Somehow, in this grey country, it gave even a cop a look of bucolic benevolence. Making the car crew a bunch of jolly fellows with no more than a poacher on their mind.

Past the Ritz, the cab slowed to the crawling confusion of Piccadilly Circus. He remembered they would need voucher, money and passport at the American Express offices. These he kept ready in his hand. The gun and keys were in the briefcase beside him. At the top of the Haymarket, the block was ten cars long. There was no time to spare if he had to be at Corrigan's by ten. It was already twenty past nine.

He leaned forward, pulling back the glass partition. "You can let me off here," he ordered, pulling some silver from his pocket.

The driver nodded without turning his head and reached back with a thick-skinned hand. The traffic had started to move. Bain broke for the pavement, just avoiding a bus taking the corner too fast. In the American Express offices, the long counter was crowded, in spite of the early hour. Bain waited impatiently while a flat Kansas accent cancelled reservations. When the man was done, Bain pushed his papers at the girl. He grinned to strip the words of offence. "Make it as fast as you can. I've got a million things to do and only one life to do them in."

She ran a crimson nail down the file cards. Pulled one and held it against the voucher.

"That's right, London–Madrid. This morning's flight. One way. You have your Spanish visa, Mr Bain?"

He flipped pages to where the elaborate signature was scrawled. "All three dollars worth."

She smiled. "Ten-thirty at the terminal, Mr Bain. Or if you have your own transport, eleven-fifteen at London Airport." She handed him the ticket.

He looked up at the clock. Twenty minutes to get from the West End to the back reaches of Walham Green. He'd never heard of Bolsover Street but Arran had said it was off North End Road. Passport and ticket grabbed fast in his hand, he groped for the briefcase. It wasn't there.

In the first moment of shock, he was conscious only of the girl's stare. As if asleep, he passed the flat of his hand across the polished wood of the counter. Then looked down at the floor.

"Have you lost something, sir?" The girl was curious but unperturbed.

Wordless, he ran for the door. He stood there while thirty cabs passed. All were indistinguishable from the one he had used. For a moment, he thought of searching the nearest cab ranks. Maybe the driver had pulled on to one of them. If not—time was going. At ten he must be at Corrigan's. In little more than an hour after that, at the airport.

In spite of the warmth, he was suddenly cold with the urge to vomit. He walked up the Haymarket, past the news vendors and into the subway. A phone booth was vacant. He dropped four coins and called Arran's number. The summons buzzed, incessant, but unanswered. By now, Arran was probably supervising the breaking up of the jewellery. His partner's caution went as far as that. He'd stand over Rojas till all that was left of the Middleburgh jewels was a heap of loose stones—a nut of platinum in an electric furnace.

Bain replaced the receiver and wiped the muck from his neck. Fear was real. Somewhere in London, his briefcase was in the back of a cab. Once turned over to the cops, it would be opened. In his mind, he could see his partner's hostile stare. Hear the quiet venom in the man's voice.

Maybe this Corrigan knew where Arran could be reached. In any case, Corrigan had to be told. Bain found a cab and gave the man double fare. It wanted five minutes to the hour when they reached the North End Road. The driver sucked a tooth. "Bolsover's somewhere round 'ere, guvnor, but *where* . . ." He gestured at the street pedlars behind their stands. "Better ask one of them."

A fishmonger in straw boater and gumboots stopped his pitch long enough to listen to Bain's inquiry. He poked a hand, wet with fish, under Bain's nose. "First right, then on your left, mate. *Fine loverly ake!*" he bawled.

Sixty-three was a five-roomed house with yellow bricks,

hideous with stained glass in the door panels. A piled garbage can stood outside the front door. Flapping a hand at the dancing wasps, Bain lifted the doorknocker. The door opened simultaneously. As though the woman had been hiding behind the curtains, waiting. She was flat-chested, fifty, and wore mustard-coloured bedroom slippers. She held the door firmly with one hand. "Yes? Oo is it?"

He was brief. "Tell Mr Corrigan someone's here to see him," he said shortly. "He expects me."

She gave him careful consideration, viewing the high brown polish of his shoes, the flower he wore, with distaste. Her mouth narrowed. "I never 'eard of 'im." She started to shut the door in his face.

He stuck his foot in the aperture and fished for the envelope. *Bolsover Street. Sixty-three.* The same number was over the door in faded Victorian signwriting. "I know," he said. "But I'm expected." He smiled.

"And I tell you I never 'eard of 'im!" She pulled the door back then shut it on Bain's foot. "I'll thank you to take your foot out of my door."

The carefully built pattern of safety was collapsing into a hopeless jigsaw. Maybe he'd gotten the street wrong, the number. "You must have heard of Mr Corrigan," he urged. "He lives on this street." He sought for words to describe a man he had never seen.

"You go and ask somewhere else," she said. "This is a *respectable* house," she added gratuitously and slammed the door.

Batting the buzzing insects automatically, he walked by the piled garbage to the sidewalk. At the corner he read the street name again. There was no mistake there. The thought of Arran possibly being at fault helped momentarily. It was best, now, to say nothing till they reached Spain. Best to do no more than run for the airport.

He was turning into the North End Road when he saw the car. It was parked in front of him. Long and with its black paint shining in the sunlight. There were bloomed rear windows that could only be used from the inside. In the front seat, two men sat watching him. He dropped on one knee, tying a shoelace. From that position, he sneaked a look behind him. A second car blocked the other end of Bolsover Road.

He climbed up, forcing his feet to take him past the car. As he drew abreast, the door opened. Two men swung heavily in front of him.

"Police officers. We'd like a word with you." The man who spoke, offered his hand as if in greeting. It held a warrant card.

Four or five women, blowsy in head scarves, stopped on the pavement. One posed a laden shopping bag at her feet, her eyes bright with anticipation. Bain took a step towards her, ignoring the cops who had moved to his side. Beyond her, a bus was rolling north, gathering speed. Just twenty yards and he'd be safe. A hundred street pedlars lined the North End Road with their stands, reducing the traffic to a crawl. By the time the police car had been turned, he could be dropping off a bus, a quarter mile away. He was close enough to the woman to smell her cheap scent.

"Go on, mate, *run*!" she shrilled suddenly. She kicked her basket at the legs of the nearer cop. It caught Bain's ankle and he stumbled, hitting the paving stones with his chest. He lay there, pinned by the detective's knees, beating the palms of his hands like a wrestler acknowledging a fall. Grunting, the second cop stood over Bain. He was hauled to his feet, one arm screwed in a half nelson.

The woman retrieved her basket and held it like a buffer. "Let 'im go!" Her face ugly, she spat the hate of the poor for the law. "Two on to one! What about them murderers! Why donchew go and catch a few of *them*?"

The detectives ran Bain through the gathering crowd to the police car. Someone inside held the back door open. As it closed, the car moved off.

Freed of the agony in his arm, shoulder, Bain slumped between the weight of the two detectives. The redhaired

17

one breathed heavily, licking a trickle of blood from a skinned knuckle. Instinct kept Bain silent. They'd found the gun and the keys. That much was clear. There was no time to think further. Between here and wherever they were taking him, he had to come up with the answer to that briefcase. It was dim behind the bloomed glass and he shut his eyes. He knew the squad car had turned east along the King's Road. That probably meant Gerald Road Police Station. It couldn't be far off eleven o'clock.

If ever you're pinched alone, say nothing. Keep your head and wait until I can get help to you.

The quiet reason in Arran's voice was a good thing to remember. Once he realised that Bain was not joining the plane, he'd be back from London Airport as fast as a car would bring him. Unless they'd grabbed Arran, too . . . Bain stifled the thought. There could be no connection between his partner and the briefcase. No chance of an arrest that might come from other circumstances. Somehow, Bain had to face the danger that he himself had produced. Above all, he had to keep Arran out of it.

The car slowed on Elizabeth Street, then turned into Gerald Road. Bain walked into the station house placidly, the two officers beside him. Bicycles were propped against the limed corridor that led to the charge room. A hatless station sergeant looked inquiry from his papers. The redhead jerked a hand and the three men went through the door marked CID.

Inside, a deal table was littered with files and three telephones. A kitchen clock clicked over an empty firegrate. A patch of sun shone through the dirty windows to the bare boards. As they walked, the dust rose under their feet. At a desk too big for the room, a man was waiting. He nodded, rapping his pipe ash in a can on the desk. He looked at Bain, his voice pleasant. "Good morning. My name's Farrell." He had a stomach that sagged and thin grey hair. "Give him a chair," he instructed.

The redhead scraped a straightback chair across the

boards. Bain sat. He watched Farrell, looking for some sign of the briefcase. There was none. He kept his eyes on the most important man in the room. Cops varied. There were the loudmouths who sought to break you with shouted confusion. A right hand swung with fury, their only alternative. Then there were the cuties, dangerous with false decency. The 'Tell me the truth, son, and I'll do what I can for you' brigade.

Inspector Farrell tamped the bowl of his pipe with a finger and lit it with exaggerated sucking noises. "What's your name?"

"Bain. Macbeth Bain." The routine was stylised to stupidity. Though you had a dossier a half inch thick, they still asked your name.

"Where do you live?" The pipe burned steadily and Farrell settled his buttocks on the edge of his desk.

"The Cloister Hotel. That's off Sloane Street." He pulled at the wood under his hands, his knees pressed tight together.

The big head moved in understanding. Under tufted brows, Farrell's dark eyes were steady. "You know why you're here, of course, Mac?"

"He knows, all right." It was the redhead, impatient of protocol. "Another second and we'd have lost him. Right, Jim?"

"That's right. He only wanted to go running off up the North End Road." The fat face creased in mock disapproval.

The smell of the place. The deadly preliminaries. These clowns and their buffoonery. All pulled Bain back to the time of his first arrest, nine years before. Nothing had changed. You walked under that blue lamp to the charge room. From there, to the dock and the cell. Jail seemed very close at that moment. Because of it, the end of all reason for living.

He knew he was tired and fought as he might. Getting to his feet, so that they were no longer looking down at him, he faced Farrell. His voice was civil. "I don't know the first thing about anything, Inspector. If this is a pinch, surely I'm entitled to know the charge?"

The CID room was silent. The laboured clanking of the typewriter in the next room clear. Farrell moved behind his desk, to straddle his chair and lean his chin on its backrest. "Have you any objection to being searched?" he asked mildly. All three cops seemed to lean towards Bain.

Content with momentary victory, he got to his feet. "Go ahead," he invited.

Farrell sucked his pipe, his eyes never leaving Bain. Once he asked: "He didn't leave anything in the car?" Both cops shook their heads. They went to work with thoroughness, searching the band of Bain's collar, the lining of his tie, his pockets. When they were done with his shoes and socks, he stood stripped, legs apart as one man probed the ultimate hiding place.

"All right! Put your clothes on." The inspector's hand played with the contents of Bain's pockets, spilling them over the desk. Keys, passport, ticket. The envelope with Corrigan's address. He opened the passport and read from it, as though to himself.

"Macbeth Bain. Born, 1922. Toronto, Ontario. Five eleven. Brown hair, blue eyes. Profession or occupation: Agent." He closed the covers. "Agent?" he asked mildly. "That doesn't mean much! Locksmith would be a better description." He held his pipe at arm's length. When the smoke cleared he was looking at Bain directly. "That was a nice job you pulled last night, Mac." There was almost respect in the challenge.

Bain kept silent. He was waiting for the briefcase to be pulled from some drawer in the desk. He knotted his tie, then pulled his arms through the sleeves of his coat.

"Where'd you leave the gun and the keys you used?"

Hope hardened at the back of Bain's mind. A trick question like that would be pointless. Either they had the briefcase or not. He shook his head. "I tell you I don't know what you're talking about, Inspector. If you've got a charge against me, make it, I know what to do when that happens. All this is so much waste of time." The clock overhead showed ten minutes before twelve. Just a few more minutes and Arran must realise that something had gone wrong.

"You've been to the hotel?" It was Farrell.

The redhead answered. "Yes. We went through the stuff in his room. Nothing there. He paid his bill this morning and told 'em that he was leaving England."

"Nothing more on the call?" said the inspector.

"Public phone in the Dorchester." The redhead was sour.

Bain let them ramble. Too well he knew the routine. The odd word thrown from one cop to another. Designed to be overheard—to confuse. Nevertheless these bums were too near the truth for his liking. How, he didn't know. But if he kept his head, he'd walk out of it. Let them be as morally certain as they liked. Without evidence, they'd never make a charge. The certainty grew that they *had* no evidence.

"I want to use the phone," he said suddenly. "If this is a pinch, I'm entitled to have my lawyer present." If Arran had taken the plane, a cable would reach him in the afternoon. If not, his partner would be at home. Ready with help when the call came.

Farrell's voice was patient. "Your record hasn't been much good since you came to England. One more con and you get the papers served on you. You know what that means!" He answered his own question. "The judge'll start at eight years. You're too sensible a chap for that sort of thing, Mac. If you want to play the game, we can do a lot for you."

The fear had gone. The picture of the cell with its saffron paint and whitewash—the barred window with tiny panes —had faded to what it must always remain. A reminder that never again must he put his liberty at the mercy of

21

creeps like these. With eight thousand pounds, the need was no more.

He lit a cigarette, killing the match with exaggerated ease. He saw Farrell with less respect. "Forget it, Inspector. I haven't just come off a banana boat. I know the game—you pulled me in for questioning. It's your hard luck that you made the wrong guess. It can happen. Even to inspectors, it can happen. You've searched me—my room —without a warrant. OK. Now let's either put up or shut up." He came over to the desk. The sun struck through Farrell's hair, pinking the scalp. Casually, Bain started to pick up his belongings from the top of the desk.

Behind him, the redhead moved a protesting fist. His partner leaned back against the door to the outer room. Only Farrell remained unperturbed. He read the address that Bain had written.

"Corrigan. 63 Bolsover Street." The chair creaked as he let his weight settle comfortably. "Did you find Mr Corrigan?" he asked.

In that moment, Bain knew that the police had been there before him. It accounted for the woman's manner at the door. How they had known he would go there was an enigma. "The man's a friend," he said, shrugging. "A friend who knows Spain. But I seem to have had the wrong address."

Farrell signalled the man at the door. "Let him go!" he ordered. "Let Mr Bain go. We've made him miss his plane, already." He stood up, his shabby bulk dwarfing the Canadian. "I wouldn't count too much on luck, if I were you," he said heavily. "If I ever get the chance, I'll put you away for as long as I can. You're just another thief to me. Worse than most of them because you've got no excuse." He let Bain reach the door before stopping him. "There's one chance in a hundred that you're telling the truth, Bain. I know your kind. If we went into court, I don't doubt you'd have a dozen witnesses to say where you spent last night. It wasn't at your hotel. But there's just that chance that you're telling the truth." He was behind his pipe again. "The Duchess of Middleburgh was robbed, last night. Whoever did it used keys and faked a window entry. We got an anonymous call this morning—a personal call to me—giving you as the man responsible. Ask yourself this, Bain. Who knew where you'd be this morning at ten? Who'd be better off if you went away for a long time? When you find the answers, come back and see me. Then, perhaps, we *will* be able to help one another."

He went out to the street, the way he had come. Past the heavy door that led to the cells. The tall desk in the charge room where the station sergeant sat, still curious. Outside the sun shone. He walked quickly. Unwilling yet to turn a head to see if he were being followed.

At Sloane Square, he called a Skyport number, and asked for Passenger Inquiries. As he waited, he watched the passers-by through the glass. Over by the fountain, a man stood in front of the pigeons, his back turned. From now on, Bain told himself, he'd be seeing cops everywhere.

The phone was alive. "Good morning! Passenger Inquiries! May I help you?"

"It's about a friend of mine," he said. "He was due to fly to Madrid on your noon flight. I'm trying to check if he made it."

"What name, sir?"

"Arran. Peter Arran. He's travelling with his wife."

"Just a moment, sir." He heard the rustling papers. "We *had* a Mr and Mrs Arran on the passenger list, sir. But I don't know . . ." Voices the other end were stifled as if a hand had been placed over the mouthpiece. "Hallo? No, sir. Neither Mr nor Mrs Arran flew. We had two passengers on the waiting list who took their seats."

He shut the door to the booth. Then Arran had to be at home. The sooner his partner knew about this past couple of hours, the better. And about Corrigan. For Corrigan was Arran's production. Bain now saw the loss of the brief-case as a chance that had saved him. And Corrigan as the villain. Only three people knew of the ten o'clock meeting. Just why Corrigan had called the cops—how he had managed to tie gun and keys to the robbery—were questions Arran would be able to answer.

He took a cab from the rank on the square. Arran's home had been chosen with care. High above a block of offices overlooking the Royal stables. On the eighth floor were a half dozen apartments where the sun lingered, early and late. To the east, the lovely stretch of St James's Park with ducks sailing their shaded water. South and west was a broken line of roof and steeple to the far hills.

He used the door on to Buckingham Gate. The scrubwomen were busy with mop and pail in the entrance hall. He remembered that it was Saturday. He buzzed the doorbell of Apartment One. He could hear the hobbled run of a woman, then the door was opened. She was tall, thirtyish, with dark hair and the deep blue eyes of a Cornish woman. She wore a small white velvet beret with her street clothes. She held the door for Bain. Once it was closed, she spoke with quick anxiety.

"What is it—an accident?"

He followed her past the four packed bags standing in the hall, into a room bright with sunshine. A painting of Arran hung over the fireplace. Twenty-five years before, the artist had caught the cold hostility in the man's eyes. Elegant in the dress uniform of the Household Brigade, the subaltern stared out at the room, implacable.

Bain pushed a pack of cigarettes at the woman. She lit one with care. "Arran's not here?" he asked uselessly. She shook her head, dark hair sliding on her shoulders. "When did you last see him?" he persisted.

Her shrug was a movement of grace. "About half past nine. He went out, as he usually does. Business, I think he said. I imagined it would be with you. We were supposed to meet at the airport." She pitched the barely touched cigarette to the fireplace. "He wasn't there." She waved a hand at the bags that stood in the hall. "*I* was. I waited another half hour. When he didn't come, I came back here." Her tone held resignation rather than surprise. But her hands were shaking.

He crossed to the window. "And you've had no message since—nothing?"

"Nothing. Last night, he didn't come home. I'm used to that. But this . . . what's happened to him, Mr Bain?"

He sought for words that would satisfy her. They lived an odd life, Arran and his wife. In two years, Bain had met the woman a half dozen times. She had seemed to accept her husband's introduction at face value.

"Caroline, this is Mr Bain. A business associate."

She had been vague without being impolite, speaking little. Most of the time, she watched her husband, nervous-eyed, as he sprawled in a chair by the open window. Once, tray in hand, she stumbled. Sending a tea cup clattering to the floor. Under Arran's stare, she mopped ineffectually, anxiety making her fingers clumsy. A second cup tipped brown liquid to seep into the carpet. Bain went down on one knee with a handkerchief. He caught the tall silver pot now threatening to topple.

Arran grinned from his chair. "Let it alone, Mac," he said softly. "Never make a woman conscious that she lacks poise."

Kneeling beside the woman, Bain saw hatred show briefly in dark blue eyes but she made no answer. When she came back from the kitchen, her grave, handsome face was expressionless. She seemed almost indifferent to the malice that still lingered in Arran's mouth.

Since he knew nothing of these things, Bain wondered how much a woman took from a man who was her husband.

She pitched her white beret to the sofa. "You haven't said anything," she pointed out. "What do *you* think happened if it wasn't an accident?"

Had he known, he wouldn't have told her. It went further than one man's loyalty to another. Arran shared secrets with no one beyond the expediency of the moment. He was jealous of any attempt to probe beyond what he cared to offer. What this woman knew of her husband's activities would be as much as Arran told her. Nothing.

"I'm trying to find out, Mrs Arran. That's why I came here. Did you ever hear him mention anyone named Corrigan?"

She sent dark hair swinging as she shook her head. "Never. But if it's important, that could mean nothing. I meet few of Peter's friends. And when I do . . ." She let the weight of her hand fall as if in defeat. "I know nothing about them."

He was becoming restless under her steady gaze. "You're sure he didn't say anything more than you've told me," he persisted. "Nothing that might give us a lead?"

She was using a thumb to roll the wedding ring on her finger. "I remember *everything* he said. He was going out on business. We would meet at the airport. He'd take his own bags." She took another cigarette from the table. "You may have noticed, Mr Bain, I never ask my husband questions."

Through the window, beyond the rounded line of the trees in the park, the traffic moved on the Mall like a line of silver-black beetles. He turned from the window impatiently. He was wasting time with this woman. Finding her resignation unnatural, he made a last effort.

"And you say there've been no phone calls since you've been back? Not from *anyone*?"

She was still staring at him. As if, he felt, she expected him to produce Arran from his pocket. "You mean the police?" she asked quietly.

He turned on her quickly, meeting a threat that he recognized.

"Who said anything about the police? I said a phone call."

A black shoulder strap shrugged free under the blue patterned silk of her dress. She pushed it out of sight. "If there'd been an accident, it *might* have been the police," she said reasonably.

Unsure of himself, he blustered. "I've got an idea that you know a lot more than you're saying, Mrs Arran. All this business about police. Well, I've got news for you. I'm not letting you make a monkey out of me. I'll find him."

"Not by going to the police, surely." The word seemed to fascinate her. She sent a second cigarette spiralling to the fireplace. "I told you I never asked questions, Mr Bain. I've had nine years' training. But that doesn't mean that I don't give myself the answers."

He stopped his pacing to stand over her. It was important that she finished what she had to say. "*What* questions?" he mocked. "*What* answers?"

The end of one pointed toe was close to his leg. She used the thin heel on his shin like a prod. "Don't shout at me! Possibly my husband has a licence to be rude. It isn't extended to his friends."

He moved away from her. "All I'm trying to do is find your husband, Mrs Arran." He matched her composure with an effort. "You'll have to believe that my reasons are valid enough."

She looked up under lashes as black as her hair. "Do *you* take me for an idiot, Mr Bain?" She took his expostulation in her stride. "The day I married, I made a choice. My husband or my family. I did it, knowing that Peter had been cashiered from his regiment. He went to prison *after* we were married. And the way that we've lived since then . . ." she smoothed the silk on her thigh. "*Business*, Mr Bain?" Her eyes were alive. She got to her feet. "Maybe I was naïve—but I believed in a new life in Spain. It mattered less how it was achieved than the fact that it *could* be a new life. I've forced myself to accept a lot in nine years. Other women—the chance that my husband might go back to prison. Why?" she asked herself. "My father would say I'm obstinate. That I've chosen the wrong bed and I'm stuck with it." She looked out across the park.

"That's not right. With money to do what he wanted, I thought Peter might change. I think it is as simple as that."

She was standing close to him. Near enough for him to be aware of the sweet sharp smell of her body, the wet brilliance of her eyes. Suddenly her hand gripped his arm, nails digging through the thin material. "Where is he?" she asked savagely. *"Where is he?"*

He let her hand stay where it was. For a moment they stood like that then she turned to run to the sofa and bury her head in her arms. Her shoulders were still but she kept her face hidden.

Because it no longer seemed to matter, he used her first name. "Caroline. You've got to listen to me. There's one man who must know what your husband did this morning. I'm going to see him now. You'd better stay here. I'll be back. If anyone but Arran telephones, hang up." She made no reply. "Caroline," he repeated. "Will you do that?"

She twisted her body, pulling down her dress where it had risen over graceful thighs. Once again, her face was devoid of expression. "I'll wait here," she promised.

He left the building and walked to St James's station. If there were a tail on him, this was the time to lose it. He bought a ticket and a newspaper from the stand. There was a two-stick report on the front page. It was a scant account of the Middleburgh robbery. An eastbound train rattled in. He boarded it and stood close to the open doors. A man in his twenties followed him into the carriage taking the nearest seat. He wore flannels and a club tie. He kept his reddened face tilted at the advertisements in front of him. The automatic doors moved under the hiss of compressed air. As they closed, Bain stuck a foot between the rubber-covered edges. Air hissed again as the doors recoiled fractionally. Bain squeezed himself sideways through the aperture. The doors closed behind him. He was facing the moving train. On the inside, the man had left his seat in an attempt to reach the platform. For a second the two men stood face to face through the glass, then the train was gone.

Hurrying now, Bain gained street level and found a cab. Twice, he'd driven Arran to Rojas's house in Hampstead. Waited outside while his partner talked. Without having met the man, Bain knew enough of the mechanics the jeweller adopted in buying stolen property. Rojas was supposed to be an anomaly among receivers. Someone who was impelled as much by artistic appreciation of a fine jewel as by greed. He bought none but gem quality stones. And as far as Bain knew, from nobody but Arran. Loot was brought, by appointment, to the house on the edge of the Heath. There, Rojas dismantled it himself. Packaging the stones in white tissue paper, he added them to the stock he collected from his safe deposit the following morning. Later in his office on Hatton Garden, he passed the jewellery to his workmen. Unsuspecting experts recut and polished caratage from the gems to make them unrecognisable. Arran's picture was of a man staled by commerce—who found pleasure in handling fine gems that he knew to be stolen. But Bain was unconvinced. For him, Rojas was in a racket and drove a hard bargain if a fair one by crooked standards.

Where the road cut across the top of the Heath, Bain paid off the cab. Up here, there was no haze except over the blue-black road surface. Unkempt brown grass, littered with paper, dipped to a copse, still green. Beyond the trees the ground climbed again. There, sweating families trudged doggedly with Saturday afternoon picnics. Here and there on the grass, lovers huddled, indifferent to the shirtsleeved groundsmen spearing garbage with sticks.

He crossed the shimmering tarmac into an avenue of elms. The thick boles were scarred with pierced hearts and initials. It was a pastoral illusion unspoiled by the tall brick wall and thick box hedges. A red setter, lying square in the middle of the road, lifted a head as Bain passed then let it fall with a thud. Twice, Bain stopped in the shelter of a tree, peering behind him. The setter lay quiet—the only living thing between Bain and the hot sunshine at the end of the avenue.

He pushed open a white five-barred gate and walked up a driveway lined with poplars. Off to the left, a racquet sung against a hard hit ball. The voices of the players were clear in the still air. The house was mock Tudor with an arched doorway and two bells. He rang both. From inside, he could hear a child calling, the kitchen noises of a meal being cleared. The maid who answered was short, dark and eager.

"*Buenos dias, señor!*" She waited, bright-eyed.

"Mr Rojas?" he asked uncertainly. Past the maid, the hall was dark. A suit of armour and helmet stood improbable sentry at the foot of a staircase.

The maid squinted in the sun, looking up at him. "*Pero no sabe, señor, si. . . .*"

A large fat man loomed behind her. His tiny feet were stuffed into white buckskin shoes. He wore gaberdine slacks and an open-neck shirt. "You asked for Mr Rojas?" he said pleasantly.

"I'm a friend of Arran's," Bain said. The air was sweet with banked carnations. He pulled the wilted flower from his lapel and let it fall to the ground.

"*Andar!*" Rojas waved one fat finger at the maid. As she scuttled, he followed her with bright button eyes. He turned to Bain. "Arran?" He lifted both hands, pulling down the corners of his mouth. "I know nobody of that name."

The frustrations of the day welled, making a snarl of Bain's voice. "You've heard of him, all right, you bastard!" He grabbed the man's silk shirt so that he felt the slack belly underneath. "*Arran!*" he repeated, shaking the man's middle. "*Madrid.* Does that mean anything? Money payable in any currency you want!" he finished savagely.

Round black eyes impassive, Rojas massaged his stomach. Then standing aside, he motioned Bain into the house. They crossed the hall into a room with stained windows. Heraldic devices gave the panelling colour. Under each shield was the name of a Spanish province. The fat man sat in his chair with care. When Bain was seated, Rojas brought both hands up, palms facing one another. He made little chopping motions, emphasising his words.

"Arran!" he said. "Madrid! I do not understand. Please tell me why you are here." The fat man's manner was too bland—too innocent to convince. Bain pushed his chair back with an abrupt movement, his voice loud. "You're going to tell me where he is!" he yelled. "I've got too much at stake to worry over a slob like you!"

Rojas settled plump hands on his stomach. "If you knew that I had business with this man, you should also know that by now it would be terminated." He watched Bain's movements with care—like a jockey watches the starting gate.

"What about if I'm in trouble—if he's in trouble?" Bain's head cocked aggressively.

Rojas squirmed, overflowing his chair. "What sort of trouble?"

"What would you say if you knew that the cops had got him. Were after him, anyway?"

Thick lids covered the bright eyes, momentarily. "There are children in this house," reproved Rojas. "I must ask you to control your voice. Why do you think that your friend is in the hands of the police?" he inquired politely.

Somehow, Bain had to break this deadlock, this pat-ball with words. He hitched his chair nearer to Rojas and leaned forward. "I know what Arran brought here this morning. I've got the best reason in the world for knowing. I know a lot more about you than you think, Rojas. But this isn't a shakedown. I want to find Arran. Somewhere, between seeing you and the airport, he's vanished. You know where he is."

"I regret it," the fat man said quietly. "But I know no more than this. I myself drove him to the airport at ten-thirty this morning. He took the airplane for Gibraltar. And there was no trouble."

Times and places made a jumble in his mind. "You mean *Madrid*," Bain corrected. "Then he took an earlier plane?"

"I mean Gibraltar," Rojas repeated. "I drove them both to the airport."

"Who, both?"

"The lady," said Rojas primly. "His wife, surely?"

"The lady," Bain repeated mechanically. He tried to say something but the words wouldn't come. Arran's face with its lopsided smile was clear. Bain fiddled with his signet ring, his watch. Both had sudden weight.

"You are ill, my friend?"

Rojas's voice was a thin solicitude from far away. Bain heard his own words with amazement, concerned at their lack of cunning. "*He* called the cops," he was saying softly. "There isn't any Corrigan." Arran had waved goodbye, sure in his mind that at ten, Bain would be in the hands of the police.

The fat man flicked ash from his white shoes, keeping his eyes on the Canadian. But Bain had no thought for him. Now that he was sure of it, Arran's treachery seemed incredible. Cold, pointless treachery. Bain searched his pockets for a cigarette, taking the jeweller's proffered light without a word. For two years, Arran had nursed him against this day. Fed him with crap about loyalty and praise for a needed dexterity with keys. Then he'd sold—not just ditched as with his wife—but *sold* Bain to the cops. For eight thousand pounds. Arran had known how Bain would react. That he would sit tight, past dock and sentence, waiting for help that never came. The end held no danger for the one-handed man. A convict would be found dead in a cell, a coroner reach a verdict of suicide. Arran had called the police, as conscious an executioner as if, gun in hand, he'd blown Bain's head apart.

He was on his feet when Rojas's thick fingers touched his

32

shoulder. They were heavy and hot. "You must not leave like this," reproved the jeweller. "You are in trouble with the police, because of Arran?"

He looked past the mask of friendliness to the fear in Rojas's eyes. "*You've* got no worries," he said bitterly. "Not yet." Hate of Arran impelled the warning. "You better take every single stone that he brought here. And sink them so deep that you forget where you've got them. If he'll sell me, he'll sell you."

He walked down the driveway to the shaded avenue. First he had to find Arran to claim eight thousand pounds. Then choke the smile from the other man's eyes. One thing he needed, an assurance that he was right.

He climbed the road to the Heath. Past the sleeping setter and waited at a bus stop. With eighteen pounds left, cabs were a luxury. He sat on the upper deck, at the back. Here he could see who left, who boarded the bus. This Farrell had to be taken seriously. Bain knew the way the cops worked. They'd be waiting for him to lead them to Arran. Then they'd settle down and wait for rogues to fall out. A cliché might be corn but it started in fact.

He looked at his watch. It was three. Arran's wife could wait. Later, he'd give her the news just the way the jeweller had given it to him. She was a big girl and would have to take her chance.

Boarding the bus, he rode to South Kensington—the subway took him to Knightsbridge. For the moment, there was no need to search the shape of every head, peer round corners. The police knew where he lived. It was when he left the hotel that he would have to take care. It was a homing that was automatic. He reached the foot of the steps, remembering that even here he might be unwelcome, now. He needed time to think about Arran's wife before he saw her. Emil was behind the reception desk. He had no smile for Bain. As Bain held out his hand for his room key, the other hesitated then gave it to him.

"Two men called this morning, just after you left, Mr

Bain," said the Swiss sourly. "They said they were police officers. When they went up to your room, I couldn't stop them. You know I dislike trouble with the police."

He met Emil's look, admitting nothing. "I expected them," he lied. "But I didn't have time to get back. There was some difficulty about my visa. I missed the plane." He tied cops and visa into an improbable bundle and dropped it into Emil's lap. "I'll be staying the night," he concluded.

"Your trunk's gone," said the Swiss, bending down behind the counter. "And a cab-driver brought this in an hour ago." He came up holding the briefcase in two pudgy hands. "The driver said he remembered picking you up here and taking you to the Haymarket. I recognised the case."

As the briefcase changed hands, the men's eyes met. Bain thumbed the fragile catch. It didn't budge. Somewhere in that cab he must have locked it and forgotten.

"I gave the driver ten shillings, Mr Bain," Emil reminded.

He threw a note on the counter and carried the case upstairs. Double-locking the door of his room from the inside, he shot the bolt. After a while, he pulled the keyring from his pocket and opened the leather satchel. Keys and pistol were still wrapped in newspaper. The case had not been opened.

He left the bed and drew the curtains, shutting out the light. It was easier to think. Moral indignation at Arran's treachery was mixed with determination to recover his share of the loot. If he had it, he would put a bullet through Arran's head without worrying about it. But Arran was a thousand miles away. To reach him, Bain needed money, a new identity and passport. Above all, breathing space. Somehow, he had to come up with a story that would persuade Farrell to remove all police surveillance. The money wasn't hard to promote. Caroline Arran had plenty. Her husband had never been niggardly with her. Her clothes, her jewellery, were evidence of it.

She was the logical choice. Of all people in London, the likeliest to finance his trip without question. He corrected himself. *Their* trip. There could be no possibility of telling her the truth. Arran had ditched her as finally and with as little compunction as he had betrayed Bain. Yet Caroline's reactions could never be the same as his. She was neither a Latin with a stiletto in her corsage nor a fanatic ready to kill for a cause. As an educated Englishwoman, she might well feel humiliation and hatred. There it would end. Background and training would stifle the urge for revenge. More than anything, a woman like that would worry about her dignity.

Yet he had to use her. He rolled over on his back, irritated by the thought. There could be no niceties of behaviour in what he had to do. It wasn't a pretty picture, using a woman's love for a man to track him—kill him, maybe. None of it was pretty. And nothing really mattered except finding Arran. If necessary, he must use anybody and anything.

Now that he had a plan, hours—minutes—regained importance. He pulled back the shades and put his head in a bowl of cold water. It was not tiredness but lack of sleep that worried him. Like a child, he blew in the water, sending the bubbles of air exploding round his ears. Then he dried himself vigorously.

It was a jungle he lived in. A jungle with your own species of cannibals. Killing a man was simple enough. You put a pistol to his head and pulled the trigger. But he had no intention of risking his own life in doing it. He wanted at once to go on living and to know that Arran was dead. First thing, he had to be rid of this police surveillance. Farrell was no fool. He'd had the Canadian passport in his hands and would know the number. It was too simple for the police to get a line on a man at any port of exit. Well, that too he'd take care of. From here on in, he'd show them tricks they'd never even heard about.

He juggled the gun and the keys in his hands. In spite of

their potential danger, he was unable to part with the pieces of metal. They belonged to him—to the moment when the sight of them would put fear into Arran's eyes. He made a brown paper package, blobbing the string knots with sealing wax. Then, unlocking the door of his room, he went down to the second floor. The phone booth there had an outside line. He dialled a number. The answer was prompt.

"Regent Messenger Service!"

"Can you send a messenger right away to the Cloister Hotel, Hans Crescent?"

"What is the name and what is the nature of the commission, sir?" The girl's voice was prim.

"I want a package delivered. I'll meet your man at the steps."

"A messenger will be there in twenty minutes, sir. And cab fares are at the expense of the client."

He waited upstairs at the window, watching the street. Thirty yards towards Knightsbridge, a seedy-looking man in a cap lolled improbably, in front of a women's hat shop. Bain kept an eye on the man as he saw the uniformed messenger arrive. Neither paid the other any attention. The messenger walked with a soldier's carriage. Bain remembered that's what most of them were. Old sweats who fetched and carried, without question, for a fee.

He ran down the stairs to catch the man just inside the revolving door. Emil's wife was on duty at the Reception desk but her nose was buried in the *Basler Tageblatt*. Occasionally, her left hand dipped into a bag of candy on the counter in front of her. The messenger stood at stiff attention.

"Regent Messenger Service, sir."

Bain gave him the package. "These are spares for a car broken down in France, Sergeant." The man stiffened still more. "I want them checked at Victoria Station." He gave the man an envelope addressed to himself care of Canada House. "Put the stub in this envelope and drop it in the mail," he instructed.

"Right you are, sir." The messenger pocketed the notes Bain handed him. "In the cloakroom at Victoria and the ticket posted to this 'ere address." He spun on his heels and went through the door to the street.

Bain stayed where he was, watching. The bum across the way paid no heed to the messenger but kept his eyes on the store front window. Bain went down the steps, waiting long enough to light a cigarette. He walked quickly towards Sloane Street. Once round the corner, he ran then ducked into a doorway. The bum came round the corner at a trot, slowing his pace too late as Bain stepped out.

"You got a match?" Bain asked pleasantly. As the other felt in his pockets, Bain held his lighted cigarette under the man's nose. "Knock it off," he said. "You tell Farrell I'll come and see him when I'm good and ready." Indifferent for the moment to pursuit, he walked back to the hotel. The woman was still behind her newspaper. "I'll be staying on for a while," he told her. "Change of plans, Madame." She nodded indifferently.

He went back upstairs. If she passed on that piece of news, the cops could believe it or not, as they pleased. In the meantime, he was going to make their job as difficult as he could for them. On the second floor, he used the phone booth again.

"Caroline. I've got news but I can't speak where I am. I'll be round in a few minutes." He hung up.

Except for a furniture truck, the street was now clear. Maybe the guy had called in a report, had been taken off. Or maybe he was sitting in the truck, peering out a slit in the side. The cops had fifty vehicles that they used for observation. Camouflaged to an appearance of insignificance. Furniture trucks, cabs, delivery wagons. Because money was no longer to be a problem, he hailed a cab and paid it off outside the Piccadilly entrance of the Ritz. Once inside the hotel, he walked through to the Arlington Street exit and took a cab at the bottom of the steps. At Buckingham Gate, he was alone in the empty corridors of the building.

The door was opened quickly. She still wore the same clothes. He followed her past the packed bags in the hall, into the room overlooking the Park.

He stood with the light from the window behind him. She said nothing but he answered her question. "It's not bad news," he said quickly.

"What have you found out—where's Peter?" she demanded. The summer's sun had browned her cheeks, leaving white the creases round her eyes.

"Sit down and listen, Caroline." He waited till she sat in her chair like a small girl. Chin up, elbows to her side. "Peter's all right. He's left word what we have to do. He flew on an earlier plane, this morning." He wanted her to help him build this lie. To ask him questions that he could smother with speed. Anything rather than a flat recital of a tale in which he had no belief.

She spoke slowly, her eyes never leaving his. "Where is he?" she repeated.

"Gibraltar. Look—this isn't the time for anything but the truth. I'll give it to you straight. As much of it as you should know, Caroline. You were right. Since I've known Arran, the pair of us have been burglars." Instinctively he sought to influence her. "Peter's your concern and I don't have to apologise for myself."

Her wide mouth was nervous. It had a trick of starting a smile without finishing it. "Why did he change his plans? Are the police after him?"

"They're not," he said shortly. Tension seemed to break in her body and her fingers pushed at the hair on her neck. "But they could be if we don't do precisely as he wants us to." He hurried the words, cautious of frightening her. "I've just seen the guy I spoke of—the one who took Arran to the airport." He turned away, trying to rob his next words of significance. "We've got to join him on Tuesday."

She seized on key words, worrying them with persistence. "Why Tuesday?"

She was taking the initiative away from him. "Because he *said* Tuesday, to start with. To give him time to make arrangements in Spain. I don't even know where he'll be till we reach Gibraltar. We'll pick up all the information we need there."

She nodded and he took heart. She seemed to have accepted the fact that they would travel together without question. "Arran left word I had to get expenses from you," he said.

She took her bag, reaching in a red leather wallet. "I've got my travel allowance in travellers' cheques. A hundred pounds. A few pounds in cash. How much do you need?"

"A hundred," he answered.

"Then I'll have to give you a cheque," she answered. She had the forms in her hand.

"Make it out to cash." He gave her a pen. "And ring your bank early on Monday morning. Tell them I'll be coming in."

She wrote with speed and decision, the signature bold. Then she handed him the pink slip, her eyes untroubled. "You will have to tell me what to do," she said simply. "If there are policemen to interview . . ." she shrugged. "I wouldn't be very good at it." She was quick to placate him. "I'm not criticising you. How could I? I'm relying on you to get me to Peter."

He put the cheque in his wallet. "You won't see any police," he assured her. "But there's one thing you'd better keep in your head. Monday night, I'll give you a name to remember. From that moment on, it'll be my name. Whenever you hear it—at the Passport Control—on the plane— when we arrive—you've got to act normally. No matter what happens." He dropped his tone to give the words force. "Not only my safety depends on it, but Peter's."

She stood up. "Whatever you tell me I must do will be done," she said quietly. "I will remember."

Always, he had thought of her as a woman without friends, relatives. No one but Arran. But he had to be sure that his lies were not to be exposed to someone less gullible than she was. "One word of what we're doing," he warned, "and the cops will have *all* of us inside. It's not a topic you discuss with your friends, Caroline."

In spite of his sombre tone, she smiled for the first time. The nervousness had gone, leaving her face tranquil. "I have no friends," she said pointedly. Then she corrected herself, giving him her hand. "I *had* no friends."

He took its warmth, finding it possible to pity her without hating her husband less. "You're going to stay here tomorrow?" She nodded. "Then we'd better have lunch together. There's plenty to talk about and Monday"—he held up two fingers, crossed—"Monday I'll be busy all day, till the evening."

"You'll have to tell me whatever you think I must know, Mr Bain.

"Mac," he said.

"Is that what Peter calls you?" Her voice was curious.

"That's what he calls me," he answered steadily. "One tomorrow, is that all right?"

She smiled. "There's food here. And there's nobody to listen."

She came to the hall with him, stopping on the way to peer into the mirror. "God," she said with feeling. "What a mess I look!" She turned impulsively. "I've grown out of practice at saying thank you. Perhaps you can imagine all the things that were going through my head, sitting waiting for you today." Her smile came ready and warm. "I've never seen a burglar who looked more like an angel. Good night, Mac," she finished.

"Good night, Caroline. Tomorrow." He rode the elevator down, alone and ashamed.

SUNDAY

HE SLEPT long that night and woke to the sound of the Oratory bells. It was good to lie there, warm and at ease in the patch of sun on his bed. He remembered, first, Caroline then his mind back-tracked through the hours of Saturday to the police and Arran.

Perhaps, more than anyone else, Arran was not to be under-estimated. He had cunning, intelligence and complete lack of scruple. Only his arrogance was an obvious weakness. "I'm never just sure—I'm always certain, as well." That had been his boast. And his confidence in his ability to outwit others must work against him. As far as Arran was concerned, he had all ends neatly tied. Bain arrested, the police satisfied with a victim. Wherever he was, Arran would read newspapers. That there was no mention of an arrest in the Middleburgh robbery would never disturb him. Time and again, he'd enlarged on police guile. He'd see no more than a plot on Farrell's part to keep the case out of the newspapers. Arran might as well have taken a pencil and struck a line through two potential threats—the police and his partner. It left his wife. A woman he must know as well as the one hand that remained to him.

The bells were finished and Bain's watch said after eleven. He started to dress slowly, taking time out to glance at the street now and again. There was the usual line of parked cars, any one of which could hold a cop. But after yesterday, it was unlikely. Even for a cop, it became pointless, following a man who knew he was being followed.

He used a towel to rub a shine to his shoes. There was no sense in letting the management know he was leaving until the last minute. As the thought hit him, he grinned. He could do better. Much better. He stopped at the second floor on the way down, calling Gerald Road Police Station and asking for Farrell. They kept him waiting. The grin lingered as he pictured Farrell having the call traced.

"CID room. Inspector Farrell," the man said at last.

Bain poured urgency into his voice. "It's Bain, Inspector. You remember—Macbeth Bain." He used the cop's cliché consciously. "You play the game with me and I'll play the game with you, Inspector."

There was obvious interest in the detective's voice. "If I give you my word, it's because I'm prepared to keep it. What's happening?"

"Wednesday afternoon, I'll be in to see you. And we're not kids. I've got a good reason for asking you to take that tail off me—at least till then. I'm trying to play a game that isn't easy. If I've got to worry about looking over my shoulder every ten yards, it becomes impossible."

"Where are you speaking from?" the cop asked suddenly.

As if they didn't know, he thought. "From the hotel," he answered. "Where I live. And don't forget—I'm not asking for favours. It's a bargain. We both want something. But it'll have to be done my way."

Farrell's voice was heavy. "I'll expect you Wednesday afternoon. And, look—Bain! You've got nothing to fear if you're not involved. If you are, you've got my word I'll do what I can for you."

He let the receiver fall from finger and thumb. There was no going back now. By Wednesday afternoon, he'd be out of the country. If not, he would have made an enemy of a cop who had friends on the force. It would be no trick for them to stir up trouble.

He took his time walking to Buckingham Gate. His mind was on the need to pump Caroline. To find out as much as she knew of Arran's original plans for Spain. Buy land cheap in the south. Build, maybe, but grow nothing. Just loaf in the sun. Beyond that, Arran had never said much. There had been a tacit agreement that Bain would stay for a while then move on. Wherever his share of the loot took him. Arran's interest in Bain's future went no farther than speculation as to how long eight thousand pounds would last the Canadian. And Bain realised that he'd *had* no plan. For too long, now, the future had been limited by the end of the week ahead.

Even that he'd viewed with indifference. Since yesterday, he recognised a change. Now, the thought of killing Arran made the future of moment. Weeks, months, if necessary, were to be used with guile and persistence. To help him on the way, he had to feed Caroline's concern for her husband. To dangle the man like bait in front of her nose.

He rang her door bell, listening to her feet click on the parquet. The way in which she opened the door wide, the warm blue of her eyes, her relaxed greeting. All these made him feel welcome in a way he had almost forgotten. The bags had been moved from the hall. She wore a blue shantung dress, high to the neck and slitted at the side in Chinese fashion.

She waved a hand at the drink trolley. "Would you like a drink before your lunch?" She seemed to move with more grace today. As if she was relaxed from the coral nails to the tips of the slim pointed shoes.

"A beer," he said, lifting the covers from the plates and sniffing appreciation. "What could be better! Chicken, tongue, ham. And a tossed green salad." He stood behind her chair as she sat. Her long hair had the sheen of a bird's wing, it's own scent.

He sat across the table from her, wondering at Arran's indifference to her as a woman. In this mood, she was a challenge to indifference. Maybe that was it. Away from the guy, she was another person. There were women like that. Ready to accept humiliation, defy convention, because of some deeper need.

Once the meal was finished, she took a chair by the window and curled her legs up under her. "After you'd gone last night," she said as though repeating a lesson, "I spent a long time thinking about you and Peter." She ducked her head, in emphasis. "A long time."

He hitched his chair to her side so that in sitting he avoided her eyes. Beyond the blowing curtains, the park was a green refuge—if you forgot the people. Suddenly he wanted to be there, flat on his back. With no worries—no need to kill Arran. Nothing beyond the blues of Monday morning and the return to a job. He pulled himself back to reality, shying at the closeness of 'Peter'. "I can understand you thinking about your husband—but how do I get into it?"

Her face was serious, propped in one hand. "You know, you frown when you ask a question. Why is that? Just like a . . ."

". . . a naughty little boy?" he asked sarcastically. He was glad of her interest yet impatient with it.

"Like a bad-tempered man," she said equably. "I didn't mean to be *womanly*. Curious, even. It's just that, since last night, I think of you and Peter together. Both of you started life with more or less the same background." She twisted in her chair so that she was looking at him. "Why do you have to fight Society—or whatever it's called—to get what you want?"

He had to control his irritation. He kept his head averted. "Look—lectures bore me, Caroline. We're going to have to fly a thousand miles together. Maybe more. Let's just accept one another the way we are."

The sound she made was more exasperation than annoyance. "Why *are* all men so conceited! I have no reason to want to change you. I don't even know you! But if you answered my question, it might help me understand Peter." She took his sleeve, shaking the scowl from his face. "I've never understood *why*, Mac. If I did, it might make things better with Peter and me."

He didn't move till she took her hand away. Then he went to the door, to the chair, back to the door. Almost as if he might worry out the answer in physical movement. His words had the weight of belief. "We're all born thieves. With those of us who stay thieves, it's a matter of motive. If more crooks start in a slum than a vicarage, it's no more than this. A vicarage upbringing is calculated to strangle all natural urges." He lit a cigarette, sending the spent match like a missile to the fireplace.

Her voice was curious. "You really believe that! That it's natural to steal?"

"Don't *you*?" he challenged impatiently. "What law isn't artificial? There isn't a single crime on the Statute Book that hasn't been extolled, somewhere, sometime, as correct social behaviour."

The lines round her eyes deepened. "But that's childish. We're not savages. At that rate, anything's natural. Even killing."

He wanted to justify himself. "Even killing," he repeated. "You give anyone a strong enough motive, Caroline, and the want to kill will be there. What stops most people is fear. Fear of what's going to happen to them afterwards. It's the same thing for a thief." He moved his hand up and down, sending tiny smoke rings from the end of his cigarette. "It's a boring topic, anyway. They've tied half a dozen labels on me, in my time. Anti-social. Psychopath. Ambivalent. Take your pick." He shrugged. "It'll probably do as well for your husband as for me."

"You don't really like Peter, do you?" she asked suddenly.

Her eyes were too aware to brook lying. "Not as a person, no," he told her. "We're partners in a business where it isn't necessary to like one another. Just trust one another."

"And you trust Peter?"

Christ, but the woman was persistent. He grinned, rubbing his hand through his hair. "Are you kidding? The guy's got eight thousand pounds of mine!"

"I'm glad you told me the truth," she said quietly. "It makes me trust you, too. I don't think anyone ever liked

Peter. He never allowed it. Not even me. I just love him."
She looked at Bain. "That's different," she finished.

This soul-baring was something you couldn't take indefinitely. "That's your business." He knew his voice to be brusque and was indifferent. "My job's to take you to him."

She acknowledged the rebuff by going to the table and starting to clear it. "You're right, of course. I should have known better. I'm sorry." She made an effort to strike a different note. "There were things you were going to tell me. Things I had to remember."

"There's little enough." It was true. Nothing to add to what he had said the night before. This gratuitous urge to see her was a danger to be recognised and overcome. "Arran's gone," he said roughly. "He's safe by now. It's only my passport that can louse things up for all of us. It's too involved to explain—even if I could. Tomorrow, I'll get another passport. It'll be false but it'll be foolproof." He talked fast, snowing her under with the force of his conviction.

She called from the kitchen. "How will we travel?"

He went to the door. She was wearing an apron, rubbing lotion on her hands. The intimacy was flattering. "By air," he said. "I'll take care of the tickets. You've got your Spanish visa. There will be no time for me to get mine. For Gib we need no more than passports."

She left her apron and followed him back to the living-room. "Don't forget to call the bank in the morning," he instructed. Money was the one weapon he needed. He felt instinctively, that it's provision meant little to her. "And while you're at it, you'd better arrange for an open credit in Gibraltar. You can do that legally. It's the Sterling Area."

She was blowing the lotion on her hands. When they were dry, she spoke, her voice curious. "What point would there be in that—since Peter will be there . . . ?"

"Who said he'd be there?" She might as well get into her head, once and for all, that Arran would *not* be at Gibraltar. "All I know is that we'll know where to reach

46

him, once we get to Gibraltar. That's not the same thing."
He hunched his shoulders. "If we need more money you'll
get it back," he assured her.

"I'm not even worrying about it," she answered. "I just
thought that if Peter were going to be there . . . You'll
come here tomorrow night?"

He nodded. "If I don't, it'll be for the best reason in
the world." He went on impulsively. "Look—if I'm *not*
here by six o'clock, go around to the Cloister Hotel, Hans
Crescent. There'll be a letter for you." He smiled with no
sense of humour. "Everything you want to know will be
in it."

As if cold, she shivered slightly. "Goodbye, then, Mac.
Be careful, at least I can say that. Goodbye," she repeated.

"I'll see you at six. Goodbye," he answered.

The hotel lobby was empty and he reached his room
without meeting anyone. Most of the guests worked in
offices. Heat and the prospect of Monday morning had
probably kept them either in the country or in bed. He
unlocked his door, listening for a while to the measured
snores from the next room. He closed the door. Nothing
had been moved. None of the maids worked on Sunday. He threw the sheets back on the bed, making it
roughly. Then he found paper and pen. There was small
chance that he would run any risk, the next day, getting his
passport. But if the deal did go sour, he intended that she
should know the truth. He wrote the note quickly.

*If you read this, I'll be under arrest. That's precisely
where your husband tried to put me yesterday. It's true
that he's gone to Gibraltar. But he's gone with another
woman. Dig yourself a hole and forget him and me. It's
the only hope you have of happiness.*

He put no signature, sealing the envelope before he had
time to reconsider the contents. He'd leave it downstairs.
Unaddressed but to be called for. With any kind of break
he would be the one who claimed it.

His bags were still unopened. He ripped off the labels. BAIN LONDON—MADRID. There were still the two spare clips for the 32. They'd be better packed. He opened the door to the corridor and listened. The harsh buzz next door persisted. He used the stairs, avoiding the centre treads that creaked, and climbed to the top floor of the building. The maids slept here. They were Irish. Probably they'd be telling beads in some church or other. He bent at each door in turn. The rooms were empty. A short flight of wooden steps gave access to the roof. He pushed up the wooden door and hauled himself to the leads. A small stone parapet guarded the flat roof. On the right, a chimney stack poked through a brick retainer. He slid a hand down behind. The two clips of bullets were in an oilskin tobacco pouch. He pushed them into a hip pocket.

Up there was a breeze that blew fresh, whipping a yellowed newspaper from one side of the roof to the other. Way off, beyond the silver sweep of the river, the roofs climbed to the heights of Wandsworth Common. Grim with grass that was never green. In its heart, the brown pile of the prison. There, a twenty foot wall shut out all vestige of summer save what could be seen through a barred window. It was the first stop on the line that finished in a jail on a moor, three hundred miles away. He turned suddenly, wetting his lips.

He made the descent with care, refastening the catch on the heavy frame. It would be as well to leave the letter in his slot downstairs. There was no sense in having it on him in the morning. He used the elevator. As the cage stopped at the first floor, he could see two men through the glass. In the lobby, Inspector Farrell was talking to the hotel proprietor. The sound of the cage brought both heads round. It was too late to press the button. Farrell had seen him. Bain walked over to the detective.

"You wanted to see me, Inspector?" As he walked, the two clips moved in his pocket. He imagined he heard the click of the nickel noses. He watched Farrell cautiously.

Afraid to draw attention to the envelope in his hands, he held it close to his side.

The Swiss was in haste to excuse himself. "Mr Bain! I didn't know you were in. I was just saying to this gentleman. . . ."

"Thank you." Farrell nodded the hotel proprietor about his business. "We'd like a word in private."

The Swiss went to his desk. Pulling an account book in front of him, he watched the two men openly.

Farrell walked Bain to the door. "I was on my way home, Bain," he said quietly. "I thought you might have something else to say to me."

Everything about the man made Bain mistrust him. His shabby bulk, the trousers bagged at the knees. The pipe he kept in his hand like an emblem of decency. Not only did Bain mistrust Farrell. He feared him. He hid both emotions. "You'd sleep easier if you knew what I was up to. Isn't that what you mean, Inspector? You'd like a reason?"

In his time, Farrell must have taken his share of sarcasm. He rode it like a swan does the backwash of a tug. "You're no fool, Bain. You've got a reason," he said with a smile.

"I've got one," Bain answered. "You've been long enough in the game to know how it is when a man shops you. Even to you people, a stoolpigeon's lower than a . . ."

"A cop," Farrell suggested gently.

Bain shrugged. The shells in his pocket no longer bothered him. This cop was smart but not smart enough. "Somebody's tried to put me inside," he said shortly. "For something I wasn't even in on. You know my form. You said it yourself—One more felony con and I get ten years. OK. I know who made that call. And why. You want the guy who pulled that Middleburgh thing. I'll give him to you. Evidence—names—the lot. You'll have them by Wednesday afternoon."

"And what do you expect to get out of it?" Farrell's

pipe was fouling the air. "The satisfaction of being on the right side for once?"

Bain shook his head. "The ten per cent offered by the insurance company," he said. "I'm a bright boy."

As if making a decision, Farrell waved his pipe. "You've got my word, Bain. I'll expect you to keep yours. None of my chaps will bother you any more."

Bain waited in the shelter of the door, watching as the cop climbed into his car, parked a decent thirty yards away. Then he walked over to the Reception Desk.

"Put that in my slot," he said pleasantly. He gave the Swiss the envelope. "A friend will call for it tomorrow afternoon if I'm not back. Not a policeman, Emil. A lady."

The Swiss poked the letter into one of the holes behind him. "Yes, Mr Bain. I'd like you to know that what I said to the officer—You've always been one of our valued guests. Never any trouble in two years, I told him."

"I'm sure he paid attention," Bain answered.

"I hope you don't think I was gossiping to the officer," the Swiss said defensively.

"I know you were, Emil," Bain answered. "But I don't mind. If I did, I wouldn't be planning to stay on here indefinitely, would I?"

"No, you wouldn't, Mr Bain. And we're glad to have you, sir."

Bain grinned. "You prove how valued a guest I am! I want a seven o'clock call tomorrow. With breakfast. Right now, you can get your wife to fix me a plate of sandwiches and a pot of coffee. Then leave me alone till the morning."

He went upstairs and pulled the shades, undressing in the half light. When the Swiss rapped on the door, Bain took the food and coffee from him and carried them to his bedside. When he was done eating, he washed his teeth and dropped a coin into the pay radio.

It was a church service. The hymn ended, there was a hawking of throats and scraping of feet as the listeners in the church settled down for the sermon. The voice was thin and cultured.

". . . words taken from the Gospel according to Saint Luke, Chapter fourteen, verses seven and eight. In the the name of the Father, the Son and the Holy Ghost, Amen."

When the coin's work was done, the clock tripped the current, silencing the speaker. But Bain was sleeping.

MONDAY

He woke alert to the business of the day. There were eight hours in which to produce a false passport. Like the rest of the half truths he'd told Caroline, need of another passport *was* important. It was a matter of routine for Farrell to call the Yard, to give the number of Bain's Canadian identification and ask for a check to be kept at all ports of exit. In a few hours, with the teletype clicking, the Special Branch would have the number in front of them. From London Airport to the east coast fishing villages—anywhere that a passport control existed—some bleak-eyed cop would be sitting, ready to crack back the word to Farrell. Holder of Canadian passport 9901 left here, bound for such and such a port.

There would be no arrest. But one signal back and another ahead. A call to the International Police Bureau maybe. Then, every time he crossed a frontier, checked in or out of an hotel, the cops would move a pin and sit back waiting for the false move to be made.

Nine years ago, when first he'd come to England from Tangier, the passport racket had been wide open. You used to meet some broken-down army major with a job at the passport office. Over a beer in a pub at the back of Westminster, you filled in a form in the name you wanted, gave the man twenty pounds and waited till he brought your passport back. . . . Inevitably, the major had grown greedy and careless. Inevitably he changed his desk at the Passport Office for the Mail Bag Shop at Wormwood Scrubs Prison. Since then, a phoney passport was a challenge to your imagination.

It was almost nine. He locked the two clips of bullets in his bags. If he were pinched for the passport—if they searched his room again—possession of a dozen and a half shells could make small difference. Downstairs, he hung his key on the hook. The letter he had written was in the slot underneath it.

On his way to Westminster, he stopped off at Cooks, Berkeley Street. "You do passports?" he asked. The man nodded. "Let me take a couple of application forms, for my wife and myself," Bain said.

The man reached behind him. "You'll need two photographs for each person. Glossy and unmounted, sir."

Bain stuffed the forms in his pocket and went back to the waiting cab. It was nine fifteen when he reached the Belgravia Labour Exchange. A stone building with echoing corridors, endless counters with grills and walls papered with notices. He tackled the man at the inquiry desk.

"I'd like to see the manager."

The man used the pen in his hand as a grande dame does her lorgnette. "In connection with what?" Under Bain's stare, he added 'sir'. Drawing breath, he asked, "Are you an employed person or an employer?" The difference seemed of importance to him.

"I'm looking for a chauffeur," Bain said. "If I have to make an appointment with the manager, it's news to me."

The clerk shed his hauteur. "This way, sir." He lifted a flap in the counter and Bain ducked under it.

The manager's office was austere. A gas stove, a row of steel files. A desk with telephone and a copy of the *Magistrates Handbook*. He kept his place in the book with a finger. His nose quivered when he spoke. "Good morning —ah—sir. What can I do for you?"

Bain sat down. "It's simple. I'm an author, looking for

a chauffeur who's prepared to travel. I can offer a job for three months. Ten pounds a week and all expenses. The man has to be able to drive," he grinned.

The man's mouth was unsmiling. "When would the employee be required to start?"

"As soon as I get tickets fixed," Bain answered. "My car's over in France, waiting."

The manager leaned his thumb on the bell push in front of him. He kept it there till the door opened. A clerk stood there, twisting his legs with embarrassment.

"This gentleman requires a chauffeur to start at once," said the manager severely. "Who do you have on the books?"

The clerk frowned. "I've got three men due to sign on at nine-thirty, sir. Possibly one of them would suit the gentleman."

"Then take care of Mr—ah——" His nose twitched. "They'll find you what you want," he added.

The hall where Bain waited was half the length of a football pitch, stone floored and festooned with NO SMOKING signs. He put his cigarette out and looked up to see the clerk beckoning from the counter.

"Over there, sir!" The clerk whispered like a stage conspirator. "Those are the three I had in mind for you."

All three men were of an age. In their early thirties. One looked bald, even at this distance. He was no good. "I'll take the one on the left, first," Bain said.

The clerk crooked a finger genteelly and the man came across the hall. Bain took a seat on the bench beside him. "Good morning," Bain said pleasantly. "I'm looking for somebody who'll chauffeur me for three months. Abroad. The pay's good and the hours easy. Have you ever been abroad?" If the man answered 'yes', it finished him there. And Bain went on to the next applicant. A man who had been abroad had a passport on record.

The man had brown hair, blue eyes and an easy smile.

"Only in the army, sir. Otherwise the nearest I get is the end of Brighton Pier."

Bain chose a car the man was bound to know. "How about a Humber?" he inquired. "Could you handle a Humber driving on the right side of the road?"

"I've driven Humbers, sir. And I've done fifty thousand miles in the army. Most of it on the wrong side of the road." The man's voice was eager.

"Can you leave in a week? What's your name?" Bain asked.

"William Ellis, sir. I could go whenever you said." He shook his head, still wearing the easy grin. "I'm one of the lucky ones. I ain't married, sir."

Bain considered. The man was the right height and colouring. He had no tattooing on his hands—no visible scars or distinguishing marks. "You'll do," he decided. "We'll tell the clerk it's settled. I'll take up your references later." As they walked across to the counter, he let the question go, off-handedly. "I don't suppose you've got a passport, have you, Ellis?"

Some of the steam seemed to go from the chauffeur. "I didn't think of that, sir. No, I never had call for one. All I got is me birth certificate at home."

Bain touched his arm. "Don't give it a thought. We'll have you fixed up in no time." He had a word with the clerk. "C'm on," he said to Ellis. "We've got a busy morning ahead."

They went to one of the Rapid Service Photo booths on the Strand. Bain watched as the chauffeur sweated under a battery of lights. They waited twenty minutes for the finished prints then Bain took the man across the street to the Savoy. They sat at a desk in the foyer of the hotel. Bain gave the man one of the application forms.

"I'll give you a hand to fill this in," he said. The man wrote, tongue guiding his pen, giving age, birthplace and description. Bain guided him through the intricacies of the passport application form. When the chauffeur made his

54

signature, he let his breath go. "Worse than driving a thousand miles, that is, sir. There ain't no more of it, is there?"

Bain shook his head. "All we have to do is pick up your birth certificate. And have these two photographs signed on the back. Who do you know who would do that for you? It has to be a doctor, lawyer, a policeman. Somebody who has known you for more than two years." A cop's signature would be ironical, he thought.

At length, Ellis's face cleared. "I've been going to Doctor Harding for nearly seven years, on and off. On the panel." He hurried an explanation. "It isn't that I'm always at the doctors. But this National Health lark, they almost force you to go, every time you blow your nose."

Bain pointed across the lobby at the phone booth. He gave the man a coin. "Ask the girl over there to get your doctor on the phone. Find out if he'll vouch for you." He smoked a cigarette nervously till Ellis returned. The man was grinning.

"That's all right, sir," said Ellis. "Doctor Harding will sign the papers for me. Said he wouldn't mind taking the job himself!"

They took a cab across the river, into the squalor of Southwark. Bain waited while Ellis ran into a seedy dwelling. Five minutes later the man came out at a jog trot, brandishing a worn envelope. His birth certificate was inside. "The surgery's just round the corner," he said. Again, Bain waited for the man to rejoin him. The two photographs and the application form bore the doctor's scrawl.

I certify that this is a true likeness of William Ellis who has been known to me for six and a half years. He is a fit person to hold a passport.

Mervyn Harding.

It was time to drop the man. He'd see him once more then never again, with luck. Bain put application form, photographs and birth certificate in his pocket. "I'll take care of all this for you," he said pleasantly. "I'll leave you here. I'm sure you'll have plenty to do. I'll come to your home at ten tomorrow. I can't give you an exact date for leaving yet but I'll know more by tomorrow."

The man stood on the pavement. Through the open window of the cab, his face was happy. "I'll wait in at ten, sir, and thanks."

Bain looked down at him. If only beating a sucker didn't leave you with a bad taste. Ah well. The guy lost no more than an identity abroad that he would never use anyway. He handed the man five one-pound notes. "An advance on the first week's salary," he said.

Back on the Strand, he had two photographs done of himself, passport size. At the same desk in the Savoy, he copied the details from Ellis's application form on the second blank that he had retained. Then, approximately, he forged the doctor's signature across the back of his own photographs. The fresh set of documents, he put in an envelope with Ellis's birth certificate and went out to the street.

Caroline's bank was on Hanover Square. He cashed her cheque without arousing comment and returned to the Strand. In a surplus store, he bought a cheap, blue raincoat to cover his suit and a peaked chauffeur's cap. It was nearly twelve, as he climbed the steps of Saint James's Park Station. The passport office was fifty yards behind. Once through the doors, the scheme seemed impossible. There were queues in front of all the counters, twenty yards in length. It was June. Every guy with the price of a ticket was trying to get out of the country.

He walked over to the wall and studied a set of regulations he knew by heart. *In exceptional circumstances*, only, would a passport be issued within the prescribed time.

He tried a girl at a desk, lengthening his vowels, clipping his word-endings in the production of some nondescript accent. "Could you help me, miss? I've got a new job, driving on the Continent. I've got to get my passport today."

"It's nothing to do with me," she answered sourly.

He resisted the urge to knock her off her chair seat. "Well, can you tell me where I ought to go?"

"Renewal or first application?" she asked.

"First application."

"Fourth floor. Room four hundred." She yawned openly at him.

Long after he had left the elevator, he carried his cap in his hand. Four hundred was along the corridor, on the left. He pushed open the door. Three other people were waiting in front of two desks. With one of the officials was a giant negress. The other two visitors stood to one side as she shouted.

"Coloured or no coloured, man. You better git ma passport before tmorro, noon. You better unnerstan that I'm British subjeck. You unnerstan it!" Shaking with rage, she pounded an ebony hand on the desk. "Room four hunnerd!" she said with scorn. "Ole securitee room! If I ain't on that boat for Trinny . . ." She poked her finger under the man's nose. "*Yaw* job ain't gonna last!"

The man nodded, his slate coloured eyes impassive. "You'll get the same treatment as anyone else, madam. Regulations are made to be obeyed and I don't make them. You bring your birth certificate in." He got up from the desk. "One other thing. This is the second day you've been here, creating a disturbance. The next time, I'll call the police." He turned to meet Bain.

Bain put his papers on the desk, cap still in hand. He knew what the room was—the woman had been right. Security. The most innocuous room in a suite given over to prying and checking. Through those doors were the files on the known passport offenders. Somewhere was the Remembrancer—a guy who sat all day pulling suspect pictures from the pile of applications, blowing them up on a screen and checking them against the mug shots of men wanted by the police.

"They sent me up here, sir," Bain said respectfully. He repeated his story.

"You want your passport today," mused the man. "That's very short notice, you know." He had a hard, ambiguous eye. "What boat are you travelling on??"

Bain hunched his shoulders. "I don't know. I got the job this morning through the Labour Exchange. My employer didn't say. All I know is France."

"*What* Labour Exchange?"

"Belgravia, sir."

The security officer scribbled on a piece of paper. He was turning the photographs over idly. "How long do you say this doctor has known you?"

"Six and a half years."

The man nodded. Then, gathering up papers and photographs, he went through a door behind him. Bain had no illusions as to what would happen now. In two minutes, they'd have the doctor on the phone. Already, Bain's hands, his back, were wet. He twirled his cap with a nonchalance he did not feel. All they could do was ask Harding if he had vouched for the application of William Ellis, chauffeur, lately employed to go abroad. Short of having the actual signed photographs under his nose, the doctor must verify his sponsorship. No mere phone check endangered a scheme like this unless something unexpected went wrong. The Labour Exchange was an unknown quantity.

He looked up as the official came back into the room. The man beckoned Bain to the desk. "Have you got your cards on you?" he asked.

The cards. He had never given a thought that they'd want to see them. Or even those he might have pulled from the chauffeur on some pretext. "Cards?" he stalled.

"Your National Insurance cards," the man said, watching him.

58

Bain looked shamefaced. "I didn't bring them, sir. I never thought of it. They're at home."

The official ignored the issue. "What did you say your job was, this one you're going to do abroad?"

"Chauffeur, sir." Bain gave him a level look.

The man's finger came down the form, pointing. "Then why describe yourself as an agent? What's that go to do with a chauffeur?"

It was there in his own writing. A legacy from his Canadian passport. He must have written it, unconsciously substituting one occupation for another. He thought quickly. "It was a toss up whether I took a job selling brushes from door to door, this week, sir. Till I got this job. I suppose agent, salesman, was on my mind."

The man pushed a pen at him. "Strike it out and put the right occupation in," he declared. "If you read the instructions on the back of the application form, you'd have seen that there are severe penalties attached to the making of false declarations." Bored, he was becoming pompous. "Take all these papers downstairs—*and* your photographs —and hand them in at the desk. Have you got fifteen shillings?" he asked as if, yet, he might be saved from issuing Bain with a passport.

"Yes, sir."

"Then get your application in before one and your passport will be ready by four-thirty." He turned away to deal with the next applicant.

Downstairs, Bain paid the fee and left his papers. At four-thirty, either the passport would be waiting for him or a couple of cops. He walked to the corner pub and had lunch, standing at the bar. Suddenly, he pushed the beer away and asked for a brandy. It was hot in the cheap raincoat and peaked cap. The makeshift uniform had served its purpose. He ate the rest of his meal with an effort, recognising the necessity of eating. He forced down potatoes that were too floury, meat whose flavour had been left in cold storage. He finished the brandy with gratitude, the urge to vomit gone. There were still four hours to kill.

He took the nearest route across the park, stopping by the deserted bandstand. People were passing on the paved walk, thirty yards away. On the grass, a few sun-starved office workers spent the rest of their lunch hour, flat on their backs. Nobody was looking in his direction. He dropped raincoat and cap over the edge of the railings to the bandstand and cut across the grass. Through the iron gate and passageway that led to Saint James's Place. The travel agency on Jermyn Street was empty but for one girl, anxious to please. She found two seats on Wednesday's flight to Gibraltar without too much difficulty. One way tickets. It was unlikely that he'd ever come back to England.

Canada House was no more than a couple of hundred yards away. The grey stone building formed the west side of Trafalgar Square. Around it clustered the Canadian banks, steamship companies and military offices. High above, on its staff, the emblem streamed in the wind, the green of the maple leaves bright against the background.

He climbed the steps into the lobby. Past the Visitor's Register and into the library. He had a word with the girl there and she ran through a sheaf of mail.

"There's just one for you today, Mr Bain." She was young, with the neat clean lines of her kind. And he knew that she was under no illusions as to who he was. Anyone who worked around Canada House came to know of Macbeth Bain, if only by repute. There were not too many Canadians in England, a source of trouble to their government.

He carried the envelope she'd given him to a reading-table and slit it open. He peeked, without pulling out the stub from the Left Luggage counter at Victoria Station.

He sat for a while, leafing a three-weeks old copy of the *Toronto Globe Mail* without interest. Occasionally a name, a face, came back to win faint recognition. In the financial section, the modest insert was still there. In the same box on the same page since his grandfather had founded the firm.

Bain, Bain and Ogilvie
Members of the Toronto Stock Exchange

Ten years ago since he'd sat at a desk in the office on Adelaide Street. Nine months after the court-martial. His father had walked, stony-eyed, into his own office. Pride of clan, of family, forcing him to hide the shame of an only son dismissed the service. For nearly thirty-six months, Bain had lived with a man to whom it was impossible to forgive. For that time, he'd sat at a junior clerk's desk, stripped of all responsibility. Worked for a junior clerk's salary. Nights, he drove back alone to the sprawling house on the Newmarket highway. They ate there in silence till his father left the room. The last time they had spoken was the day Bain had returned home, an ex-lieutenant in the Royal Canadian Navy. For almost three years, the two men lived like that until the frustration was too much to take. Then came the night when there were eight thousand dollars in his father's safe. His parents asleep, he'd crept downstairs, silencing the two Dobermans. Nuzzling his legs, they'd followed him into the dark library. Past the shabby leather chairs to where the safe key hung in a dirk scabbard on the wall. For an hour, he'd sat in the dark, the wet-nosed dogs at his feet, the money heavy in his hands. Then he packed two bags and drove all night to Montreal. At that time, the wrong of his act, its shabbiness, had been a memory that he forgot in a parade of bars stretching from Paris to Rome. It was in some third-rate rooming house in Marseilles that he woke, nine months afterwards, broke. From that moment, he'd lived without regret. Sure, now, that he had no more than taken a patrimony that was rightly his.

He pushed away the newspaper and went out to the lobby. As he passed the stairs, he saw Ferguson on his way down. In twenty-five years, that carrot hair and freckled face had changed little.

"Hallo, Mac!"

Four years in school, three in the navy—Bain had spent too much time in the other's company not to sense more than just surprise in the other's greeting. Odd, the way things fitted in. More than anyone, perhaps, Ferguson belonged to that memory of Bain's parents. Once, it had been Ferguson who stood in a Tangier bar, a bottle in his hand and a dead man at his feet. It might have been yesterday. The tiny square, high in the Medina, the walls reeking with ammonia. The bar with its bead flyscreen across the door. And behind the zinc, a barman who still swabbed mechanically. Over in a chair, Sharley the guide, his face olive with fear. And Bain.

They'd been two junior officers off a destroyer in the bay. With Fergy, whiter than his drills, a broken bottle, splintered where it had crushed the Arab's forehead.

"Mac—the bastard tried to knife me."

It was more than a plea for understanding. It was a pop-eyed kid who'd carried Bain's skates, asking for help. Bain reacted instinctively, grabbing the bottle, pushing Ferguson through the door ahead of them. They ran through the stinking courtways and alleys, a yelling chorus of Arabs after them. At the launch, the International Police were courteous but adamant. Then came the night in the cells with the inspectors alert to the cuts on Bain's hands. Two frightened Arabs identified Bain as the dead man's assailant. In the face of Ferguson's silence, his own refusal to deny guilt, Bain had been charged. It was the last year of the war, with few major powers ready to surrender a serving officer to the International Zone of Tangier. The signals that passed between the destroyer and Gibraltar ended in court-martial and dismissal.

The years had treated Ferguson easily since then. If he remembered, he never mentioned. Yet such times as they met, his official disapproval of Bain's career was often belied by the half-spoken word—the sympathy incompletely expressed.

"Hi, Fergy," Bain said. "And how are Her Canadian Majesty's consular representatives this morning?" It was always easier to be banal than to risk memory of an event best forgotten.

The sandy-haired man looked up and down the corridor. Then he opened the door to an empty office. Both men went in. "We were talking about you in the HC's office, this morning, Mac."

Bain leaned the backs of his legs against the desk behind him. "Yes? Then nothing to my credit, I want to bet."

Though there was nobody else in the room, Ferguson lowered his voice. "I shouldn't tell you this but we had a call about you, upstairs."

Bain nodded. "The police?"

Ferguson used his finger to trace a pattern in the dust of a typewriter cover. His voice was embarrassed. "It was the same old thing. A couple of times a year. Whenever you're . . . " he showed white, uneven teeth in a grin . . . whenever you're on temporary leave of absence from jail, we get a call from the cops. It's all very smooth and British. They're either checking your birthplace or the date. But the guy's always eager to get any little bit of information about you that we're ready to hand on. This morning, it was some character wanting to know the number of your passport."

"And?" said Bain. Farrell might keep his word according to the letter but that's as far as it went.

Ferguson shook his head. "I took the call. I told 'em nothing. All right, we represent Canada here. But the way I see it, our job's got nothing to do with police work. That's for Ottawa."

"Thanks, Fergy," Bain shrugged. "It didn't matter. They've got the number anyway."

"Ah," said Ferguson and lifted a hand. The clock across

the square struck the hour. He spoke impulsively. "You don't want to go back at all, Mac?"

"Where?" Bain made the other answer. His grin was sour and he had no regrets.

"To Canada."

Like a benevolent fox, the guy was, Bain thought. He shook his head.

"Christ, I know it isn't my business." Ferguson frowned. "Yet I'm pretty sure things at home could still be patched up. Both your mother and father are getting on. It isn't as though there's anyone else to take your place. Jeannie and I saw them both when we were back in the spring. I'd do what I could, Mac."

"Would you?" asked Bain. "*Would* you, Fergy?" The question was answered in Ferguson's eyes, just as Bain knew it would be. Ten long years, sweating it out in the consular corps, with maybe a plum short months away—you didn't pipe up loud to a confession of murder, all that time ago. And for what! To save a guy like Bain who'd loused his life up anyway. "I'll tell you what you could do, if you really want to help me, Fergy."

"Anything I can," the other said uncomfortably. He kept his eyes unwavering with an effort.

"Then ring back Scotland Yard," said Bain. "This guy who called you this morning. Tell him that you had my passport here for renewal. That I brought it in today. Use any excuse you like but get that over clear to them."

"And *then* what?" asked Ferguson. "I've got nothing to do with passports really. That's Cronin. What's he say if he gets to hear this and doesn't have your passport?"

"He *does*!" said Bain. He tossed his Canadian passport on the desk. "It isn't due for renewal but I want it to sit here for a while. These cops are crazy, Fergy. I want them off my back for a while. It's important to me that they're sure I'm not leaving the country for a bit."

The other man sat, looking down at the blue folder in front of him. "I'll do it," he said suddenly. "I'll call the guy back and pass this on to Cronin." His thin face was young as he smiled. "It'll be a month in that office of his before somebody realises that the thing's not out of date at all."

The two men stood together for a second, uncertainly. Then the redheaded man's voice was diffident. "Nothing else I can do?" He opened the door of the office, accepting Bain's head shake. "So long, Mac, and good luck." He went up the stairs.

There was still time to waste. At the top of Lower Regent St, Bain ducked into the cool of a newsreel theatre. For an hour he watched snatches of news, irritated by the phoney drama in the voices of the narrators. The lighted clock showed five minutes to four. He bought a package of gum from a girl in the aisle and went to the lavatory. In the stall, he stood on the seat and stuck the cloak room ticket with gum to the underneath of the cistern cover. The shells were one thing. This stub would claim pistol and keys and not until he was out of the passport office would he be safe.

By the time he reached there, the building on Petty France was about to close. Grilles were up at all the windows save one. He took his place in the queue.

The man had no time to waste. "Name?" he asked mechanically.

"William Ellis," Bain answered.

"Ellis?" repeated the man testily. He looked through the pile of buff envelopes on his left. "When did you make your application?"

"This morning," Bain answered. There were no cops springing from behind pillars. Just the indifference of a man who had never heard of you. "I had to go upstairs. Room 400." The clock on the wall was loud. Through the space, the man's eyes seemed hostile, aware. Fear jumbled Bain's thoughts. Could he have run, he would. "I'd better come back, then," he said uncertainly. He wanted to get through the doors that were now being locked. Run before he had to jog through empty corridors, heart banging a hole in his chest—behind him the cry "Stop him!"

"Room 400," the man said. "That's different. You only made your application today!" He spoke as though this were a personal discovery that made everything clear. He picked an envelope from the smaller pile on his right. Opening the passport, he looked at the photograph inside.

"William Ellis," he said and handed the passport to Bain.

He kept his legs straight, his eyes on the door ahead. It was thirty yards, with every sense impelling him to turn his head and face the danger that must come screaming from behind. The doors had been locked to allow only those in the building to leave. As Bain neared, the commissionaire swung them open, relocking them after him.

Not till he'd reached the corner, did he find courage to open the envelope in his hand. He did it hesitantly, as a bomb disposal expert might tackle a time fuse. The stiff blue covers were slightly sticky and bright with gilt. The cheap photograph was like a mug shot. All it needed was a number hung across the chest. He looked inside the cover.

Her Britannic Majesty's Principal Secretary of State for Foreign Affairs requests and requires in the name of Her Majesty all those to whom it may concern to allow the bearer to pass freely without let or hindrance and to afford the bearer such assistance and protection as may be necessary.

He put the document away safely in an inside pocket. Then he cut across the park again and into the newsreel theatre. In the lavatory, he retrieved the stub. It was after five when he rang Caroline's doorbell. This was a woman whose husband you intended to kill. Yet you stood there, listening for the sound of her feet in the passage. All he needed, he thought sourly, was a bunch of flowers in his hand.

She had dressed in a shade of blue that heightened the

brilliance of her eyes. She shut the door quickly and he walked into the hall, watching the play of her thighs as she moved in front of him. She sat in her favourite chair and tucked her chin into slim fingers.

The feeling of importance she gave one was good. Her fine ankles together, her scent sharp with femininity, she perched there as if this were the moment that made her day. He swaggered a little, everything forgotten save the desire to impress with his cleverness. He let the passport dangle from finger and thumb. "There it is," he told her complacently. "William Ellis. From now on, I'm William Ellis. Can you remember that?"

She moved her head seeming to accept his cunning without wanting to understand. "And there's no danger?"

He leaned back on the sofa, crossing his hands behind his neck. "Danger? Not the way I do things, Caroline." He screwed up his eyes as if in strong sunshine. "We leave tomorrow morning. Ten-thirty at the airport, Channel 4. Don't come near me—don't recognise me—till we're through Customs and Immigration. Once we're on the plane, I'll see that we sit together."

She watched his mouth as he talked, nodding or shaking her head as he made his points. "I'll get you some tea," she said quickly.

"I've got things to do," he answered. This intimacy was too dangerous. The wish for her approval too strong. Sitting there, across from her steady gaze, the softness of her throat, he wanted nothing but the sense of her friendship. He risked forgetting the part she had to play in his plan. Already, he'd tried seeing her as an adjunct to Arran— co-relating her to his partner's treachery. It hadn't worked. For she was a victim, no less than he was. What he had to do was to think of her as a means to an end. Only she made the thought intolerable by her readiness to like him.

"Tomorrow," he said and went to the door.

"Tomorrow, Mac." She gave him her hand.

"This time, it won't be a wasted trip," he assured her, smiling.

"I know." Her face was less strained. She touched her hair, smiling back at him. "I know," she repeated and closed the door.

In the hotel, he took the letter he'd written together with his key. Once upstairs, he tore the note to shreds and flushed them down the lavatory. In bed, he dozed fitfully, half erect at the sound of every cab that drew up, nearby. Chain smoking till his tongue burned in protest. His mind raced, producing doubt after doubt, rejecting each one in the same instant. Finding Arran was the toughest proposition. Yet Gibraltar was no more than a rock with twenty streets—a half dozen hotels and an airport.

He shut his eyes tight, recalling every trick his partner had ever used—the way the man had met every emergency over the past two years. Arran used his caution like a smoke screen, obscuring his activities from the police, his wife, his associates. But once he felt no need for caution, he became as predictable as the next man. Off-guard, even more predictable. For he never relaxed with any but his own kind. He travelled as they did, aspired to the same level of living. At the airport, in the best hotel in Gibraltar, there'd be somebody who would remember a tall, grey-haired man, missing his right hand. That was wrong. They'd remember Arran as a gentleman. A man friendly to servants without being familiar, whose quiet courtesy to his inferiors hid the menace reserved for their betters.

Bain stubbed the last of his cigarettes and rolled over on his side. He slept as he had done since a child—knees drawn up near his chest, one hand covering his mouth as if to silence it.

TUESDAY

HE WAS up, shaved and dressed before the maids were moving in the corridors. He carried his bags down and left them in the hall. Then he walked over to the passage behind Knightsbridge Green. In a truck-drivers' hangout, a bleary-eyed woman gave him hot strong tea and damp toast. He drank the brew, his stomach rebelling against the stink of fat bacon, frying. By the time he reached the hotel, it was eight-fifteen. Unshaven, the Swiss was at his desk, the collar of his pyjama coat peeping above his jacket.

"Let me have my bill!" said Bain. "I've got exactly half an hour to catch the Edinburgh train." He shrugged. "I knew nothing about it till late last night."

The Swiss added figures then took the notes Bain proffered. For a second, his face showed the resentment he had hidden for days. "An assignment, Mr Bain?" He shut the cash drawer tight and pocketed the keys.

"Just that," Bain said. "You know, Emil, I could grow to dislike you easily. I never knew how easily." He leaned over the counter and the Swiss moved back hastily. "Tell your friends this," said Bain, "whenever they come round. I'm going to Scotland for six months. And if they give me any more trouble, I'll make a stink that will reach even the Home Secretary's nostrils."

He found a cab and gave the driver Ellis's address in Southwark. Bain kept the vehicle waiting and went across to rap on the chauffeur's door. The man opened it himself.

"Good morning, sir." Ellis was hesitant. "I'd ask you in but I only lodge here."

"Look, Ellis." Bain made his voice friendly but regretful. "I'm afraid my news isn't good—about the job. There was a cable waiting for me last night. It means that I have to fly to the States today." He threw a hand at the cab. "I'm on my way now."

The ready smile weakened then finally vanished. "You mean you're not going to want me after all, is that it, sir?"

"I'm afraid that *is* it," said Bain. "Not for a couple of months, at any rate. I'll drop you a line as soon as I'm back. If you're free then . . . I'd like to have you." He made a wad of five one-pound notes and pushed them into the other's hand. "The other half of the first week's wages, Ellis. If we never do get started on that job together, keep the cash for a drink on me."

It took a few seconds for the man's resiliency to assert itself. Then he looked up. "OK, sir. Thanks very much and good luck."

From doorstep to the road grating at the kerb was a half dozen feet. Bain covered them before stopping as if remembering. "Hey, I've still got your papers," he said. He gave the man back his birth certificate. The photographs, the form Ellis had completed, Bain kept in his hand. "You're not going to need these for a while," he grinned.

The man neither understood nor cared. It was obvious. "No, I'm not, sir," he answered.

"Then that's the best place for them," said Bain. He ripped the papers across and dropped them down the grating. "Easy enough to do it again if we need them." He got back into the cab. "So long," he called through the open window.

"So long, sir," echoed the chauffeur.

Bain took the cab back to Victoria Station. It was nine fifteen. In front of the gates for the south-bound trains to the coast, queues a hundred yards long were forming. A party of military police stamped across the concourse. Between them, a frightened youth, capless but in uniform. Bain shoved through family groups surrounded by their baggage and bawling children. He found the Left Luggage counter and presented the voucher.

"Sixpence to pay. Two days at threepence," said the attendant.

He carried the flat heavy package out through the side entrance to the station, into the offices of the car hire company. The big Armstrong Siddeley made the entrance gates of London Airport in forty-five minutes. The driver screwed his head round.

"North or Central, sir. Where are you flying to?"

"Gibraltar, BEA. That's Central," Bain answered.

They drove out of the bright sunshine into a tunnel, deep under ground level. In front of the two main buildings, the driver pulled the limousine into one of the bays. Already, the baggage handlers were at the trunk of the car. Bain squared the driver.

With the intensity of movement around him, his uncertainty seemed to go. Four planes circled overhead, waiting their turn to touch down. On the edge of the tarmac, vehicles scuttled from end to end. Service jeeps, ambulances, passenger tenders. Air crews swung out of the building, haversacks in hand. Hindus in dark blue uniform, Swedes, Germans, Americans. The trim behinds of stewardesses hailing from California, Czechoslovakia.

Ahead was a lighted sign: GIBRALTAR 11 hours Flight 123. He walked across and watched his bags weighed. The girl ticked his name on the passenger list and smiled pleasantly. "That's all the luggage you have, Mr Ellis?"

He held up the package. "Nothing else," he told her.

She gave him back his ticket and passport. "There's five shillings airport tax, sir. Channel 4. Upstairs and to your right."

He went up the elevator to the Main Hall. Leaning against the coffee bar, he looked round. Even now, he half-expected Farrell to spring from behind a pillar. The airport was always full of cops of one or another variety. Big florid men from the Flying Squad, a fraction too well-dressed for policemen, meeting a plane on a tip-off. Or maybe just passing an hour on the off-chance that they might fluke a familiar face on its way out, in a hurry. The Special Branch, less obvious in their cloak and dagger act, ready for the troubled in spirit without the necessary visa. At least twice a week, somebody was marched off to the small red-brick station house along the highway. Usually, it was the diamond smugglers. Rabbis with beards, elderly ladies with intermittent heart failure, unsuspecting children. All had been used as carriers. All had been sunk by the one trip too many—the careless rendezvous—the rat-squeak of a police informer.

There was no one he recognised except Caroline. She was making her way across the hall towards Channel 4. She carried a small square box in one hand, her bag in the other. She wore the blue dress, the white velvet beret making her hair as black as pitch. As she passed him, her eyes moved in brief recognition but her head never turned. A lady about her lawful occasions, he thought with admiration. He left the coffee and went round the corner to the florist.

"An orchid," he ordered, choosing a flower with the delicate veining of rose marble. Wanting the gesture to remain a surprise, he pushed the Cellophane-wrapped bloom into his pocket.

Over in Channel 4, the seats and tables were occupied. The air shrill with Gibraltese Spanish. Cool, alone, Caroline Arran stood by the entrance to the Customs sheds, staring out through the window. He moved away. By the National Provincial Bank counter, he smoked a cigarette, his eyes alert for the unfamiliar. The public address system barked above the clatter of voices.

"Will Mr Ellis, passenger on Flight 123, London to Gibraltar, please come to Channel 4 immediately!"

Twice, he listened to the girl's voice with no more than the faintest interest. Feet across the way were shuffling. The passengers for Gibraltar moving through the door. Package in hand, he ran after them. There was no Customs examination. He waited on the end of the line that had to pass the battery of tall desks. Behind each was a plain clothes cop attached to the Special Branch.

"Are you a British subject?"

He realised the stewardess was talking to him and nodded. She shepherded him to a desk. He waited in front of it, trying to stifle the feeling of guilt that he felt must show in his eyes, his every gesture. The cop flipped the pages of Bain's passport, glancing at the list in front of him, ticking the last name.

"Mr Ellis?" he queried. His eyes were bird-bright as if eager to spy the smallest chink in respectability.

"That's right," Bain answered.

"Thirty-two." The cop checked the number of passengers with the stewardess. He slid the passport across the desk to Bain.

Inevitably, his hands felt fat and troubled. It would be better. With every frontier that he passed—every stamp they rammed at the blue folder. The fear of detection would go. A phony passport had two flashpoints of danger—leaving or entering the country of its origin.

The passengers crowded into the waiting room. There were no more controls. Nothing but a bus between here and the Viscount, a quarter mile out on the tarmac. A sudden rush and England would drop away beneath him.

Caroline was still standing alone. He walked across to her. "That's that," he said quietly. "You were great. For a second you had me wondering whether you knew me or not."

"I knew you," she answered. Her eyes were bright with tears. They rolled unheeded, making her cheek-bones shiny.

The other passengers were moving down the glass-enclosed ramp to the bus. He gripped her elbow tight, hurrying her after them. She ran awkwardly, knocking a little at the knees. He took the square case from her hand. "Now, what, for God's sake?" he panted.

She made no answer, wiping the wet from her face with a handkerchief. In the bus, she answered him—as if she

73

might destroy him with the words. "The faithful friend," she said bitterly. "All those lies for a hundred pounds."

He grabbed her wrist till the rough gold of her bracelet cut into his palm. "What do you mean?" he snarled. In the seat in front, a woman turned her head. Bain lowered his voice. "*What?*" he demanded.

She pulled a letter from her bag and gave it him without more words. Recognising Arran's handwriting, he pulled the paper from the envelope.

London Airport

Dear Caroline:

By the time you get this, I shall have left England. You're not joining me now—or at any other time. I have no wish for it. In case you're in doubt, you should know this—I've gone with another woman.

Too many years of your bloody forbearance have given me the taste for something a little less virtuous.

The flat, what money there is in the bank, they're all yours. I suggest you go back to Cornwall and enliven your respectable father's declining years with tales of my villainy.

Peter.

He turned the envelope over. It had been mailed the day Arran left. With the intervening Sunday, one sorter's slip accounted for the delay. He gave her the letter back, searching his mind for a lie big enough to smother the others.

The bus stopped. At the foot of the gangway, she waited for a second, the hair on her neck swinging in the draft from the turbo-jet. Then she walked up the slope to the plane. Bain sat next to her. "Well," she asked him. "No more quips? No more lies?" She fiddled ineffectually with her seat belt. He helped her, feeling her cold hands. He could no longer lie yet he had no heart for the truth.

She talked slowly, in a small voice, as if to herself. "I should have known. Peter bothering to send someone to bring me to him. It could never have been true. Never. It's just that I wanted to believe it. That's it. I wanted to believe it." She sat, unconscious of her fresh tears.

The two stewardesses were making the last transfer of papers at the end of the aisle. A port motor roared as the pilot gunned it. There was still time. The gangway had not yet been withdrawn. He started to undo her seat belt, half-turning to halt the stewardess. "Get out of here, Caroline," he said impulsively. "Get off before the plane starts!"

She pushed his hands away, shaking her head. "What did he do to you?" she demanded. Though her face was still wet, there was no tremor in her voice. "I've known what I had to do ever since I had that letter," she said. "It's too late. For me. For you. For Peter."

There was the flat sound of a door being hermetically sealed. Then the motors screeched and Bain was glad that talk was useless. The plane lurched slightly, shuddered then screamed for the end of the airstrip. A gentle bump and they were in a world of rushing wind.

Bain eased the metal clip on his seat belt and pushed the lever by his side, tipping his body back. The vent over the port deflected cool air on his forehead. He shut his eyes. He didn't know how he could handle the woman beside him. Arran's letter was a gratuitous salvo—an off-hand malevolence against which no precaution might ever have been taken.

If Bain hadn't made it possible, Caroline wouldn't have left London. He'd given her a good enough reason for the journey. Arran's letter provided her with a better one.

He pulled himself up in the seat. She sat erect, hands gripping the ends of the arms rests. He touched her fingers tentatively. They were cold. She kept her head averted, indifferent to his touch. He knew he must say *something* to her. He was beyond bluster. Eager to give her comfort yet unable to part with the whole truth. Instinctively he felt her a menace to his plan. Killing Arran was a thought he accepted now, much as he accepted one day following another. Inevitable but without drama.

"You want excuses," he said slowly. "I'm past them. All right, I lied. The way *he* lied. The way you'll lie when it suits your purpose, too." He felt her body move in protest and she shook her head blindly, eyes closed tight. He tightened his grip. "I say *yes*! We're all in this thing for strictly our own ends. You better understand what's happening—before you get carried away with this picture of yourself as a figure of tragedy."

She used her hand mirror. Dabbing her eyes, her mouth, the corners where traces still showed of her tears. Then she snapped the catch on her bag and turned her body so that she faced him. "That's the sort of thing you say because you think it's weak to be anything but bitter—callous. I'm under no illusions—I know exactly how little I matter to any of you. That's not the point, now. For the first time in my life, *I* want to have something to say. Why are *you* making this journey?"

He shifted in his seat, muttering. "I've got good enough reason. There's nothing that bastard wouldn't do to someone he feels stands in his way. You—me!" He hunched his shoulders. "That's beside the point. He's got money of mine. I want it."

She leaned nearer as if determined that the truth should not evade her. "You never knew he had left England?" she demanded.

He kept his eyes on the seat in front of him. "A letter took care of you," he said bitterly. "With me it was a phone call that he made to the police. For once, the luck was with me. It back-fired."

"God!" she said quietly. "And when you see him what will you do?"

He couldn't trust her. If the three of them were there, she'd take the gun from his hand to protect Arran rather than kill him. Even if he were wrong, this vengeance was a personal thing that could never be shared. The need to protect it made him cunning.

"I want what's mine. Nothing else," he lied. "When I get it, I'll never see him again as long as I live. That's my reason, Caroline. What about you?"

Uncertain of each other, yet bound in conspiracy, they sat silent till the stewardess had gone by with her tray. "Loyalty for you is something to do with your liberty—nothing more," said Caroline. "You expected me to sit alone in that flat, decently resigned. Just as Peter did." She was controlled but implacable. "I've had enough of being pushed around. I'm going to be less virtuous. *Less virtuous!*" she remembered. "Christ, how I hate him!"

A hand came back from the seat in front, brandishing a slip of paper. Bain took it and read the words without interest.

Flying at 23,000 feet. Approximate speed 285 miles per hour. Over the Bay of Biscay.
Captain Bishop.

He pushed the paper into her hand and got up. She was a danger. Somehow he had to get rid of her. Because he needed time to think, he took the package from the rack overhead and walked aft to the lavatory. Once inside, he put the gun in one hip pocket, the keys in the other then washed his hands. He went back to his seat, sure in his mind what he had to do. But he was unhurried. He lit a cigarette, and watched the clouds beneath, for a while. They were like balls of raw cotton, soft and without substance. Caroline sat with her chin in her hand, staring out at the endless blue.

He brought his mouth close to her ear, his voice quiet but definite. "I'll tell you where you're going, Caroline. Back to London. Just as soon as I can get you on a plane. You've got no part in any of this. You just think you have." Without bothering to answer, she made the shake of her head as determined as his words. He stabbed his butt into the ash tray. "All right! We'll do it the hard way. You're on your own, once we land in Gibraltar." Irritated with her obstinacy, he tried ridicule. "How far do you suppose you'll get, by yourself? Where are you going to start looking for him?"

"Stop it!" she said suddenly. "*Stop it!* I meant what I said. I'm tired of being pushed about—disposed of. You *won't* leave me!"

Hysteria, he thought, and let the implied threat go for what it was. The truth came easier now. "Sooner than let you make an even bigger mess of your life, Caroline, I'll leave you all right."

She shook her head again. "You won't, *Mr Ellis*."

He remembered the passport and wet his lips. He watched her eyes, trying to hide his fear behind a grin.

She spoke to him gently, almost with pity. "It isn't hard to be ruthless. You ought to know that. If you force me, I'll tell the police who you are." Her hand touched his arm. "Listen to me, Mac. You've got to help me find Peter. When you do, he's yours first. You must take your money and go. Go as quickly as you can and forget about both of us." She shook his sleeve. "I don't know how sincere you are. I feel that I no longer know about *anything*. But I'm not your responsibility. I'm not," she repeated.

He tried to find fresh argument. Her proposition was too logical. "All right!" He stuffed his hands deep in his jacket pockets so that she would not see that shake in his hands. His fingers fastened on the flower, crumpled but still in its Cellophane. "Here," he said awkwardly. "The lies had nothing to do with this."

She held the flower loosely. For a moment it seemed as if she would let it fall to the floor. Then she unwrapped the orchid and pinned it on her shoulder. "Is it a bargain?" Her voice was friendly.

He nodded, unafraid of the inquiry in her eyes. It was a bargain that he would keep to the letter. If Arran was dead when her turn came to see him, so much the better for all of them.

He dozed beside her till the feeling of falling brought him upright. He looked through the port. They were beneath the cloud ceiling, banking in an arc that flattened in line with the great rock ahead. A sign lit up at the end of the cabin.

FASTEN YOUR SEAT BELTS
NO SMOKING

They buckled the clips round their middles. The plane lost height rapidly. Then the violet mass of the rock rushed at them. He had a brief impression of grey ships in deep blue water, the white and tan buildings, and they were down, the undercarriage nuzzling the tarmac. Very slowly, the plane rolled to a halt in front of a haphazard collection of sheds.

He took Caroline's square case and followed her down the gangway. Outside, the heat hit viciously, blurring the sharp outlines of buildings fifty yards away. Over the Control Tower, the windsock bellied with sudden wind, then flapped listlessly. After the green of England, the colours were harsh and unfriendly.

They filed into the shed. He gave Caroline her case, taking the place ahead of her. If the police asked tricky questions, she could get her cue from him. The line moved slowly, between railings, into an office. Three policemen waited there behind a desk, inspecting the passports. They wore old-fashioned tunics, buttoned up to the throat. Two of them, squat and olive-faced, had the air of masquerading. The third was fresh-faced and spoke with the slow burr of a Norfolk man.

"How long do you intend staying in Gibraltar, sir?"

"I don't know," Bain answered. "It depends. Three or four days probably." It was long enough. If Arran were here, he could be found in that time. If not, they were wasting precious days on the Rock.

The officer stamped the passport and handed it back to Bain. "Do you know where you'll be staying, sir?"

"That depends, too. The Rock Hotel, probably." He took the slip the man gave him and read.

RESIDENTS ORDINANCE, SEC. 4. CAP. 53.

Name: Mr W. Ellis.

From: (ship or aircraft)

B.E.A.

is permitted to enter Gibraltar and reside *night(s)*: seven.

EVERY PERSON MUST REPORT TO THE POLICE REGISTRATION OFFICE AT GENERAL POLICE STATION, IRISH TOWN, FOR REGISTRATION OR RENEWAL.

A. L. ABRAHAM.

Gibraltar 7. 6. 57.

Scrawled across the top of the page in schoolboy's handwriting was 'Rock Hotel'.

"If you stay longer, sir, apply to the police station."

As Bain went through the door, he heard Caroline's answer. "I'm staying a week, officer."

The Customs officer had heavy gold braid on his cap and a choleric manner. "Which bags do you say? These two, sir? Right! What have you got to declare?"

"Nothing," Bain said. He expected no Customs examination between London and Gibraltar. Both were in British territory. Both in the Sterling Area. In one of the two bags were the shells for the automatic.

"No firearms, explosives?" asked the man, severely. He had his nose near the end of Bain's bag, his red face redder with exertion.

"Nothing," repeated Bain.

The man was already interested in Caroline's hand case. "Open this one, miss, please."

Bain waited for her beyond the barrier. On an impulse, he went to the phone booth and called the hotel. "I'd like to speak to Mr Arran," he said.

The clerk was unhesitant. "I'm sorry, sir. Mr Arran left yesterday."

They found a cab, glad of the cool air rushing through the open windows. It forked left at the cross-roads where a sign pointed west—SPAIN. They drove under the arch, past barracks where kilted soldiers sweated across the blistering square. Up the narrow, main street—a procession of Indian stores, glittering with junk. Past Governor's House to the steep hill.

The hotel was long, white and cool. Carved from the rock, the gardens were terraced down to the road. A porter carried in their bags. The reception clerk had dark skin and an assessor's eye. "Rooms, sir?" He ran a finger down a chart. "I can do you a double with bath."

On the impulse, Bain sent Caroline to a chair where she waited quietly, her ankles crossed like those of a small girl. "Two singles with baths," he said.

"And for how long?" The clerk poised his pencil.

"I called a little while back, from the airport." Bain talked on the hunch. "Asking about Mr Arran—he's a friend of ours."

The two passports were open in front of the clerk. "Would the lady be a relation of Mr Arran's, sir?"

"Sister-in-law," answered Bain. "We'd hoped to meet him here. How long we stay rather depends on whether he's in Gibraltar."

The clerk looked up from the business of copying details from the passports. "Mr Arran left yesterday. With the lady. We booked rooms for them at the Minzah Hotel in Tangier."

"Ah," said Bain. "Then there's probably a message for us somewhere. We'll stay only one night, then. Can you get me seats for Tangier?"

The clerk snapped his fingers and gave two keys to the baggage man. "Three-one-four and three-one-five," he instructed. He returned his attention to Bain. "How do you want to go, sir? Bland Line ferry, direct to Tangier—the Spanish ferry from Algeciras, across the bay in Spain. Or by plane. We can book passage for you on any one of the three."

"Two seats on tomorrow morning's plane," said Bain.

"Two. Very good, sir. I'll have your tickets ready this evening."

It was a big room with a balcony. A connecting door, locked on Caroline's side, was bolted on his. Beyond it, he could hear her moving about. He showered, shivering with delight under the cold water. When he was done, he sat naked in a chair for a while. Then he took the two clips from his bags. In future, these would go with him, in his pockets. The weight of the gun sagged in his hand. The oiled blue steel was dull—the scored butt heavy. He worked the trigger rapidly, a half dozen times. Then he fed the clip into the gun, pumped one shell into the breech.

A cane chair creaked on the balcony outside. He took the white towel robe from the bathroom and stepped into the sunshine. The floor of the balcony burned his bare feet. Caroline was on the other side of the railing, slim, nervous fingers gripping the balustrade. Hearing him, she turned. In that bright light, the fine lines round her eyes were more pronounced. She smiled at him. There was less greeting in her face, he thought, than resignation. The gaiety of the past two days was gone. Had he known how, he would have comforted her. Instead, he lit a cigarette and perched on the dividing rail. Without talking, he pointed south, across the Straits. Fifteen miles away was another continent and Tangier. Since the morning, neither had mentioned Arran. But Bain never forgot.

The curve of the Spanish coast—the blazing bougainvillæa in the gardens beneath—the smell of Africa on the wind. It meant that he would kill Arran in more exotic surroundings. Nothing more. In Bain's mind, there was nothing beyond the picture of Arran's face. An unready face, full of fear. There could be no shot in the dark or from ambush. Arran had to know why he died, who killed him.

"That was kind—what you did downstairs." She looked up at him, shading her eyes from the bright sun.

"The day I'm caught being kind, anything goes," he said. Both her hands were up now, like a visor. The softness of her arms touched him. "But I like hearing about it. What was my particular good deed for the day?"

She left the balustrade and came near him. "Wanting to spare me the sordid details," she answered. "About Peter and the woman he stayed here with. It didn't matter, but it was kind, just the same."

He grinned. "If you twist my arm, I can do even better. Taking you out on the town, for instance." He ticked off his fingers. "The museum. Three cinemas known locally as flea-pits. And, unless things have changed since my day, a joint where you drink warm beer, and watch an old crone do the can-can and avoid the falling bodies."

She smiled at him. "It sounds terrible. Were you here in the war?" He nodded absent-mindedly. "Doing what?" she asked.

He stepped hard on the cigarette butt. "I was a hero," he answered. "A goddam heroic hero." Without excuse, he went into his room and lay on the bed. Sometimes the memory hurt. A chance word tripped the mechanism and back it all came. Like a newsreel seen a thousand times. He balled the robe and threw it at the bathroom, glad of the wind on his skin. Any moment and he'd be sorry for himself. Bain, the victim of circumstance. He pulled the pillow over his head and lay still.

It was eight o'clock when he tapped on her door. She was in a black dress caught at the waist with a narrow gold belt. She held his arm, all the way down to the restaurant. Her fingers barely touching the stuff of his jacket, as though unwilling to impose. They ate in the fashion of people who know one another well. Content for the while with one another's company. He walked her back to her room, unwilling that this comradeship should end yet with no idea how he might prolong it.

He sat on his balcony in the hope that she would come out, pitching one cigarette after another into the night.

When the light no longer showed in her room, he undressed and walked barefooted in the dark. From door to balcony, turning endlessly as he had done in a cell. Restless, he took the gun in his hand and unloaded it. Fifty times, he clicked the trigger rapidly, wheeling in the dim light, the butt pressed tight against his stomach. Till, satisfied, he recharged the weapon, pumping one shell into the breech, ready for firing.

A tenth of a second could make the difference between his life and Arran's.

WEDNESDAY

WITH THE new day, he went out to the balcony. Down in the gardens, sprays whirled, the water making the grass greener than life. A tiny rainbow hung in front of one spray. Sounds were clear. A bugle in the town—a steam hammer in the naval yards. It would be another hot day.

He paid their bill then went to the terrace to eat breakfast with Caroline. She no longer asked how he took his tea but poured the brew for him, strong and sweet. Often, she smiled at him suddenly, without apparent reason. Not understanding, he was disturbed. She was wearing a dress without sleeves, no stockings and her head was protected by a scarf tied French-fashion. He'd have been happier in shirt and slacks but the bulge of the gun made the jacket necessary.

He wiped the egg from his mouth. "Are you fit?" he asked.

She nodded without looking at him. She was using the mirror in her bag. Something about the hand that held it seemed wrong. He realised she had removed her wedding ring. For a day, now, she'd puzzled him. She spoke vaguely about things yet with determination. What she thought she could do to Arran, for instance, was a mystery to Bair.

Caroline mentioned her husband as one does an enemy. Bain watched her follow the curve of her mouth with a stick of red. All these things, she did with an economy of movement that was good to see. Maybe, he thought, it was possible for a woman to meet a man who had humiliated her—to wreck him with words and still retain her dignity. Whatever she did would be *done* with dignity, of that he was certain.

"I'm ready, now," she said, looking up. All the nervousness in her mouth was back, belying the calm of her manner.

A cab was waiting in front of the portico. The entire way to the airport, they sat quiet. Like people who drive to a funeral, he thought. Once, his hand burnt by the hot leather seat, he moved it. He was touching her fingers. Without exaggeration, she gave his hand the quick squeeze of a child for a puppy, letting her fingers stay there.

"Has anyone ever told you," she asked. "You have the gift of making people feel wanted?"

They forked left to the airport. He could see the frontier post. The police sign HALT. The Spanish sentries, ominous in their German-type helmets.

"No," he answered. "Nobody ever told me that before."

They went through the passport control and took their seats in the plane. There were fifteen passengers. A few British; an American couple; a group of Moors, dignified in grey linen *djellabahs*. The pilot took the short passage across the Straits low enough for them to determine the colours of the flags the ships flew. Beyond Point Europa, blue water met green. On the Spanish mainland, tiny puffs of white smoke burst from the coastline to land in the clear air, expanding into dirty grey clouds.

"Coastal batteries," Bain said, remembering. "You never know whether it's just a fiesta or an attack." He leaned close to her, pointing at the stepped white roofs that rose from the waterfront. They came in low, from the north, the crooked alleys of the Medina beneath them. One last lazy swoop and the plane settled down on the airfield. Grass pushed from the cracks in the tarmac. Beyond the barriers that led from the field, a mob of Arabs milled around, shoving and shouting.

He took Caroline's elbow. "This is it," he said quietly. "We can't be sure he won't be at the airport. If we do see him, let me deal with him first. That's the bargain."

He used his shoulder to make his way through the yelling baggage carriers. There was a tall Arab with a fez and a grey beard who stood behind the others. Bain called him and the man came, running. He kicked and elbowed his way to Bain's side.

"You speak English?" Bain asked.

"Understand," said the Arab and touched hand to heart, mouth and forehead. He took off his fez to show a shaven skull that gleamed in the sunlight.

Bain pointed at the luggage on the truck. The Arab took two cases in his hands and slung two on a strap round his neck. His deep voice bellowing for room, he went ahead of them. There was no Customs control, no more than police waiting behind a counter. They were not alone. Three or four guides lolled familiarly at their side. The passports were given dual inspection. One of the police stamped the document and the guide at his shoulder retrieved it. After he, too, had studied it, he claimed the owner as a client. Already the Americans ahead were having trouble, the man arguing with the guide who clutched the green passport as if determined never to relinquish it.

Suddenly Bain froze. Then he walked slowly, lifting his feet like a dog who sees a cat. Behind the counter, at the side of the next cop, was an enormous fat man. He wore no hat and tight, oiled curls sprang like wire from above his ears. He leaned on the cop's shoulder, one plump hand guiding his words into the official's ear.

Bain pulled Caroline in front of him, holding her as a shield. "Cover me till we get past this fat guy," he said quickly. "Don't ask questions, just do it!"

The people behind pushed, moving Bain slowly past the cop and the fat man. As he passed, he ducked his head, presenting no more than a shoulder. Three more yards and they would be at the end of the line. Another cop waited there.

The fat man had finished his confidences. He pulled a lilac-coloured handkerchief from a green gaberdine jacket and blew his nose heartily. His head turned towards Bain. Then he peered round Caroline's body, muddy eyes perplexed. He spoke in English.

"Passport, meester!"

The cop nodded, holding out a hand. Bain pushed the passport across the counter. His body next to hers, he could feel the girl tremble. The officer ogled her openly. "And Mees, passport!" He kept his grin fixed on Caroline, ramming the stamp at the passports haphazardly. The fat man retrieved them. Holding the two booklets high above his head, he came round the barrier.

"Follow, please, lady and gentleman. Follow, please!" He used his great stomach like a bulldozer, ploughing his way across the hall to where the porter waited with the bags.

Caroline stood uncertainly. "Come on," said Bain. "It doesn't matter now."

Eleven years had gone by but he remembered every line in the guide's face. It was a day that had started with the pair of them, Ferguson and him, at the waterfront. That's where Sharley the guide picked them up. A day that finished high in the Medina with Ferguson standing over a dead man. The fat man had been one of the two to testify that Bain had struck the blow. All that was past but remained the matter of a passport in the name of Ellis.

They walked out to the hot concrete. The bearded Arab was already stowing the cases in the trunk of a Packard limousine. Sharley directed him with lordly sweeps of a bolstered hand then threw the man a few coins. He ducked his head at Caroline and gave her her passport. "Sharley, mees! A good guide and very honest. Meester Ellis," he said to Bain. "I am happy to see you." He held open the door of the car and climbed in after them. He sat opposite, resting one enormous buttock on each of the occasional seats. "*Now!*" he said, showing teeth like a cat's, "we are old friends. What can I do for you?"

Bain moved quickly, taking his passport from the guide's hand. "You get in my hair again, Sharley, and I'll kill you!" On an impulse, he kneed the other's weight off one seat and took it himself. He rammed the end of the gun into the man's soft flesh, keeping his voice low. "What's my name?" he demanded. In front of them, the driver's head never turned.

The stink of the fat man's fear was above the scent he used. "You are Meester Ellis," he said in a small voice. "I ask only to be of service. A good guide and honest," he finished mechanically.

"Please, Mac." Caroline made a move as if to block the gun in Bain's hand.

He shoved it back in his pocket. "Let me take care of this," he gasped. He was breathing heavily and he wiped the sweat from his forehead. "I know this bastard." He grabbed a fat ear lobe and twisted it savagely. "We're old friends, you heard him!" He let the man go. "Tell the driver to take us into Tangier. *Slowly.*"

The fat man mopped his head, then spoke to the driver in Arabic. He sat erect, watching Bain apprehensively. The car moved off and Bain went back to sit beside Caroline.

He stabbed a finger at the guide. "I'll tell you about him," he said heavily. "Sharley's a man who knows everyone in Tangier. He'll get you a whore in five minutes or a shirt made in an hour. He knows who slept where for the past twenty years here and hasn't an enemy in the town." He kicked and the fat man drew in his ankles hastily. "But he's a weasel-hearted liar. Aren't you?" he demanded. "*Aren't you?*"

The dull eyes disappeared behind thick lids and the man bent his head. "By God's name," he said, "it has been on my conscience. I lied but I did as I was told, Lieutenant Bain. I am a humble man."

"You're a dog," Bain answered. "A dirty, pariah dog. Who told you to lie—the police?"

"They were sure," the guide said in a whine. "I tried to tell the truth and they beat me."

"Mac, *please*!" urged Caroline again. "I don't know what all this is but be sensible."

As always, anger left him weak. He lit a cigarette, trying to keep his hands steady but they shook all the more. If anyone in Tangier knew where Arran was, it was the guide. Sharley met every boat, every plane into the city. To use him would be just that—sensible.

He pointed a finger at the guide. "I'll give you a deal," he said sombrely. "I'm looking for someone who flew into Tangier yesterday morning." He described Arran. "There was a woman with him and they went to the Minzah Hotel. I want to know how they use their time. Where they eat, walk, sleep. In the meantime, you'll find us a place to stay where we'll be out of the way. Play straight for once in your life and you'll be paid." He nodded his head. "If you don't, you'll be paid, just the same."

The fat man's face flushed at the menace. He hurried to placate Bain. "This **was** an Englishman with lady. Young and like Mees, very pretty." The gallantry was gruesome. "They left this morning on the ferry for Algeciras."

The car turned off to the main highway. Incapable of holding down speed any longer, the driver put his foot on the accelerator. They were going through a Bidonville— a shanty town where the dwellings were made from flattened gasoline cans. Hearing the car, curs rushed at the road, chiyiking. Three scabby-eyed children ran a few steps, half-heartedly yelling for alms.

Bain lowered his head into his hands. If only he could stop the pulse that beat in his temple, ease the pain. Always

Arran was one move ahead. Sure and indifferent to pursuit. The next move might take him out of reach.

They turned up a cypress-lined avenue. White villas sprawled under red roofs, the only Arabs servants, spotless in cream robes. They passed a polo field, a group of players hacking towards it. They were nearing the town.

"Tell the driver to stop at the Minzah," Bain said wearily. "I want to know where that Englishman's gone. Not just Algeciras but *where*—an address. If you tell me tonight, you'll get twenty pounds. Tomorrow, fifteen. The next day, ten. After that, your information isn't worth a nickel."

The car circled the Place de France and turned down the narrow rue des Statuts. In front of the hotel, the fat man opened the door. "I shall order your rooms." His eyes were still apprehensive. Bain nodded and some of the guide's assurance came back. Walking like a man testing rotting boards, Sharley went into the hotel. In five minutes, he was back, a couple of bareshanked Arabs following him. "It is done." He opened the door for them, his sagging shoulders an expression of humility. When Caroline and Bain had passed, he inflated his great stomach and roared instructions at the porters.

Inside, the hotel was like a court in a mosque, cool and tiled. Beyond the desks, an arch led to a patio hung with brilliant creepers. Tables and chairs were set round a fountain that played into a basin. Sharley waited until Bain and Caroline signed the register. Then he touched Bain's arm.

"At six o'clock, you shall have the information you seek." He tapped his chest, lifting his two chins proudly. "If this is possible, I shall be the one to do it."

Bain shrugged. The guide was no longer a threat. Fear and cupidity evoked a temporary loyalty that the fat man would respect.

"I want a visa for Spain, as well. By this evening. Can you do that?" he said.

The guide took Bain's passport. "My wife's cousin is

doorkeeper at the consulate," he said simply. He put one hand on his chest and ducked his head. "Till six o'clock, gentleman, lady."

Caroline moved her body so the draft from the fan overhead caught her neck. She held the long hair away from the damp tendrils. "Can you take me shopping for an hour?" she asked the guide. "Come back here for me at three." She turned to Bain. "I'm going up to my room."

He stood for a while, uncertain, watching as she walked to the elevator. She was able to disturb him with a gesture. Sometimes, he felt he recognised a significance beyond what she said. He took the guide's lapel, tugging it gently. "Tell me where the lady goes," he instructed. "Whether she sees anybody. If she sends a cable, I want to know what it says."

Bain let go the man's coat. The guide smoothed the material fastidiously. "It will be done," he promised.

They took their lunch in the shade of the inner courtyard. If she had further interest in Bain's past, she controlled it. Upstairs, he had hoped that she'd continue to question him. Now, her indifference was a challenge. A half dozen times, he started to meet it only to tail-off under her level stare.

At three, the guide arrived and Bain was left to finish his coffee in the patio. The memory of this city—all that had happened because of one night, eleven years ago—was too strong to resist. He went out to the street and down to the market place. Arabs squatted behind mounds of melting goat's butter, piled fruit, bargaining from the dirt with shrill cries. He walked by the stands covered with tooled leather-work, over to the story-teller's corner. An ancient man kept his audience spellbound beyond the filth and the noise that surrounded them.

He walked down es 'Siaghine, ignoring the offers of the money-changers at their booths. Shoving through the letter-writers, the gossips who sat on the bottom steps, he started the endless climb to the Sultan's Palace. The way was narrow and unpredictable. Sometimes overhanging balconies almost touched. At others, blank whitewashed walls offered uncompromising shelter to the curs at their base. Left and right, still narrower passageways zigzagged up or down.

He pumped his legs mechanically, the weight of the gun and the keys irksome. Slipping on the fouled cobblestones, he kept going up. Then the tiny square was in front of him. At its end, the café with its beaded curtain at the door. Everything was as he remembered it. Even the old man who nodded on the kerb in front. There was a smell of burned pepper that hung to one's clothes. Hashish. Bain looked at the old man on the kerb. A pipe with a tiny bowl was at his side. The two yellow dogs sniffed at Bain, scratched themselves vigorously and went back to sleep.

He turned away, damp yet satisfied. The place was a stinking monument to a gesture that ended disastrously. One that Ferguson chose to forget and of which others only remembered the disgrace. He clambered up the last two hundred steps to the palace. It was the highest point in Tangier. He was alone. In the heat of the sun. He sat on the wall, looking across the straits. Spain was no more than a dark broken line beyond the bright silver of the water. Somewhere behind those mountains, Arran was happy in the sun.

The wind came in suddenly from the sea, bending the acacias, whipping the dust into eddies at his feet. He started down the steps. It was six by the time he reached the hotel. Sharley was waiting. Seeing Bain, he came to his feet clumsily and combed his hair. "It is done," he said, bringing his mouth close to Bain's ear. "All is done!"

Bain pushed the man away. "You stink of garlic," he said. "I hear you well enough. Where is he living?"

The guide struggled the passport from an inside pocket. "First, the visa," he said, with satisfaction. "There is a little extra charge." He waved his short arms. "Such speed is not usual."

The visa was good for three months. Inside the stiff covers was a perforated card with six tickets. Each was good for either one exit or one entry into Spain. "Where's he living?" he repeated.

The fat man joined both hands in front of his chest. "Please, first listen! Then say whether I have done well. The Englishman went to the bank of Moses Imossi. Here he took a great sum of money in American dollars and pesetas. A car was to meet him in Algeciras." He paused for approval but Bain was giving none. "It will take him to the Miramar Hotel in Malaga. Is it well done?" he finished anxiously.

"Well enough," said Bain. There was always this pattern. Arran twenty-four hours ahead. A sudden move and a hotel for one night. The more time that passed, the more chance that something might disturb Arran's complacency. Then the carefree tourist would turn into a man capable of disappearing under Bain's nose.

Bain took twenty pounds from his pocket. "How much are you going to stick me for the visa?" he asked.

The guide held up four fat fingers and a thumb. "And by my father's head, I swear I am not covered!" He crept closer to Bain's ear again. His eyes cunning, he whispered. "For five pounds more, I have important information."

Bain searched the man's face, trying to gauge the truth. "For five, let it be good," he answered.

"The lady bought a pistol," Sharley said softly. "I showed her where she might do this. A small pistol but deadly, sir." He shook his head. "She spoke to nobody. No cable."

Bain stuffed the notes into the guide's hand and ran for the elevator. He padded up the corridor to listen outside Caroline's door. There was no sound from inside. His hand covered the door-handle. He turned it slowly, then threw all his weight at the door. He half fell into the room and stumbled across to the bed. In spite of closed shutters, it was light enough to see her lying there. As she heard him, she rolled over on her back, stuffing a gun beneath the pillow. He ran back to the door and locked it.

Eyes adjusted to the half light, he saw that her face was wet. "Give me that gun, Caroline!" he said.

She stayed where she was on the bed, like a dog that expects to be beaten. But she kept the gun. "No!" she whispered.

He moved towards her cautiously, talking to her, watching her hands all the time. "You've got to give me that gun, Caroline. I want to help you."

Cradling the gun in her two hands, she shook her head. Her voice was louder—more definite—"No!"

He grabbed her wrists, forcing her to drop the gun to the bed covers. She broke free. Making fists of her hands, she fought savagely, battering his neck and his face. Blood started to run from his nose but he held her tight. Suddenly, her fingers clawed his neck. "Help me!" She was beyond tears, desperate. "*Please* help me, Mac!" she pleaded.

He sniffed the blood running back to his throat. Lowering his face, he kissed her as he had always known he would. With tenderness, yet aware of the warmth and softness of her body. Holding his hand like a lifeline, she pulled him down beside her to the bed.

"What was the gun for?" he whispered. He leaned his cheek against her hair, squeezing the shake from her shoulders. "You've got to tell me. Was it for me, for you, or for Arran?"

She sat up straight to touch the blood on his nose and cheek with her fingertips. She fetched a wet cloth and wiped them clean. For a while she stood, looking down at him. Then she bent and kissed him on the mouth.

He took the pistol and pushed it into a pocket.

"Answer me!" he demanded. "I'll help you but tell me!"

Her fingers were in his hair, cool and comforting. "I was going to kill him." She seemed to wonder at her words. "It was the only thing I could do."

He knew what she meant and held her tighter. Her

intentions were in the past. All this woman had ever needed was to be wanted. He took both her wrists in his hands, pulling her down so that the softness of her breasts was on his neck.

"But not any more?" he asked.

"Not any more," she promised. She looked at him again. He sensed rather than saw the appeal. "You swear that you'll help me, Mac?"

Lost to the desire to comfort her, he swore, out of pity. After a while, she went over to the shutters and closed them completely. He sat, head bent between his hands, as she undressed behind him. Then she said his name, twice. He let his own clothes fall to the floor and got in beside her. His lips met hers and all the bitterness of the day was gone.

He slept—to wake disturbed. Her head was dark on the pillow, facing him, eyes hidden under a veil of hair. She didn't move as he left the bed. He dressed and went to the windows. Opening the shutters, he stepped to the balcony. In the light from the street, he could read his watch. Nine-thirty. The city was a jumble of dark roofs, splashed yellow where the lamps burned. The air was heavy with a hundred smells—exhausted.

As he came back into the room, something whined by his cheek. He unhooked the mosquito netting over the bed and started to lower it. Caroline stirred, shaking her face free of the blue-black hair. Then her hands came up to meet behind his neck, pulling him down to her. Unwilling, he shrugged himself free. He sat on the edge of the bed, conscious of her firm leg against him, knowing that she was watching him.

He burnt a match, lighting a cigarette, stalling. She was waiting for him to speak and he had nothing to say. When she touched his wrist with her fingers, they were no longer cool but hot—imprisoning.

She yawned. "What time is it?"

He found his voice, glad of the banality of her words. "Twenty-five to ten. We'd better eat. You get dressed." He got up and stood looking down at her. His every nerve was alert for the claim she must make.

But she yawned again, lifting her chin and stretching. "Wait for me downstairs. I'll be twenty minutes."

Irresolute, he made as if to touch her shoulder. She caught his hand, gripping tightly. "Twenty minutes," she promised.

Back in his own room, he set about changing. Clean linen, another suit. He used the shower, shocking himself with cold water. Then he dressed. On the bed were the things he had emptied from his pockets. Passport, money, keys. Now two guns. He released the catch on the small Browning he had taken from her. The magazine was empty. He locked both weapons in a bag and went downstairs.

She was sitting alone at the horseshoe bar. Her back brown against the white linen dress, she studied the bottles behind the counter as if they were of importance. She wore no jewellery save an enamel watch. He took the stool beside her, watching her carefully in the mirror in front of them.

"Poor Mac!" she said suddenly. Her reflection smiled from the mirror. "You look so harassed! There's no need," she said quietly. She looked into the bottom of her glass, her eyes hidden.

He shifted his weight with discomfort. *For Chrissakes, say it!* he wanted to shout. *Say whatever it is that I've got to listen to and get it over!* He ordered a drink and swallowed it, indifferent to the bite of the brandy.

"What did you do with the shells to that gun?" he demanded.

She looked up, the angle of her head, the smile, like those of a small girl solving a riddle. "That's why you're pulling those horrible faces!" She opened her bag. The barman stood fifteen feet away, polishing glasses. Dipping into the white skin bag, she pulled out a cardboard box and dropped it into Bain's jacket pocket. "Here," she said quickly.

He shoved his glass across the bar and watched irritably as the man poured. "More!" he instructed. The barman substituted another glass with a flourish and filled it. When the man was gone. Bain tried to make his tone authoritative. "Look, you've got to stay here in Tangier, Caroline. It can only be better for both of us. There's no longer any need for you to see your husband. What *I* have to do can be done twice as quickly if I'm alone."

Her answer was to take the edge of one nail and scratch it gently along the back of his hand. "If you drink all that on an empty stomach," she said, "you'll fall flat on your face. And I'm not good at dead lifts."

He half emptied the glass deliberately. "I'm going to have a sandwich here," he decided. "You go in and eat. I'll wait here for you. Did you hear what I said?" he demanded.

"I did," she said composedly. "I'll eat a sandwich with you. You'd better get used to the idea of me being where you are, Mac. Unless you don't want me," she added. Though nothing aided her eyebrows, they formed one straight thin line when she drew them together. "Are you sorry?" She made a point-blank issue of her words.

He ordered some food, using the barman as a buffer. The challenge had come. He watched her with caution. Her mouth was sweet, her eyes kind. But they could have no real meaning till her husband was dead. And to kill Arran, he had to be free of her, if only for a while. He tried for the right words, desperately. "Sorry for what?" he said.

She pushed the plate of sandwiches in front of him. "Don't scowl! she smiled. "Are you sorry about *us*?" There was no coyness in her voice but deadly seriousness.

He told himself that every gesture she made, every word, implied possession. It was a threat to a life that had never known that sort of complication. He answered her honestly. "No, I'm not. It isn't that and you know it. There are times when a man has to be alone to do something. This is one of them." She gave no encouragement, waiting for him to go on. He broke a sandwich moodily. "Half the time, I don't know *what* I mean. How I feel. You don't know what you're taking on. I'll never change," he challenged.

She lifted a hand. "I don't want you to," she said quickly. "Except perhaps in one way. I want you safe. If it didn't mean so much to you, I'd say forget Peter. Just as you told *me* to forget him. I have means enough to take us a long way away." She shook her head. "It won't work, will it? I know how you feel about Peter and this money. I'll help you get it, Mac. I won't be a nuisance. I don't want to see Peter. Ever. But I want to be with you."

He ate mechanically, without tasting the food, washing it down with the raw spirit. For the first time in many years, being self-sufficient wasn't enough. If this woman got up and walked out of his life, some of the sense of living would go with her. How long it could last, he didn't know. But the future didn't stop with Arran's death. It started with Caroline.

She leaned across, indifferent to the barman. She took Bain's cheeks in her two palms. "What difference can it make?" she whispered. "He'll be afraid. He'll give you the money, quickly. It isn't as if you'll be running from the police. I'll even stay in another hotel. But you can't leave me here," she pleaded.

There could be no more argument. Deep down, what he wanted was Caroline on his terms. And she was ready to accept them. All except one. Fear closed his mouth so that she would never know it.

"All right," he said. He put his cheek against hers, glad that the choice was made. "We'll need money." He counted the notes in his wallet. "I've got barely twenty quid left."

"We'll cash these travellers' cheques of mine at the desk," she said with decision. "If we need more, we can use the credit in Gibraltar." She hooked her hand in the crook of his arm. "Now, cheer up. Nothing's finished. It's beginning." For the first time, she said "Darling!"

He pressed her hand, wanting to believe in her words. They went to the patio. A bright Milky Way arched across the night, dappling the purple with silver. Every star seemed to be out, this evening. They sat on the edge of the fountain. Caroline trailed her hand in the water. The pale fish scurried for shelter.

She was not looking at him but spoke with her head bent, as if asking the question of her reflection. "Where shall we go when you get the money?"

He didn't want to answer. All he remembered was that this thing would be between them as long as they lived. Without her, the memory of Arran would have been a fierce joy. He had wanted to live and Arran had condemned him to death. Instead, it would be Arran who'd go. The memory should have stayed like that. Without dramatics. Now the man's death would rest an affront. Something of which Bain must be ashamed for the rest of his life.

She was still playing with the silver slips in the water. "Where will we go?" she repeated.

"I don't know," he said slowly. "The Caribbean, perhaps. I'm getting sick of running. Maybe there'll be some hole for us to dig there. Anything. I dunno," he said again.

"I think I'd like that." Her head was averted. Her voice quiet, considered. "Yes. And I'd try to make you happy, Mac."

In the starlight, her skin was dark gold. She was near enough for him to smell the sweetness of her body. He wanted to take her and told her. To blurt out the truth and feel the gun taken from his hand. He forced Arran's face into his consciousness, answering her with impatience.

"That's asking for trouble. Being dependent on someone else for happiness."

She shivered as though with a chill. She got to her feet. "I'm cold," she said improbably. "I think I'll go to bed."

He walked her to the elevator. As they went down the corridor, he grabbed her arms, pulling her mouth to meet his. His fingers were digging into her flesh and she winced in pain.

"You've got to be patient with me," he said. "I need you as much as you need me, Caroline." Inner conviction gave certainty to the words. "As soon as we get to the Caribbean, we'll be married."

She put her cheek swiftly against his. "I'm not going to be locked up for bigamy." She used this glad laugh rarely. "I'll have to divorce Peter first, remember?"

He turned the key in the lock, holding the door open for her. "With luck, he could have an accident," he said sombrely. Even now, he was unsure how deep her hatred of her husband went. He gave her his hand, finding a smile to reassure her.

She snapped the light button in the room. The bed had been made, the mosquito curtains drawn. "Peter doesn't have accidents," she said after a second. "They just happen to the people around him." Once more she held up her cheek. "Good night, Mac." His name was an endearment, the way she said it. She closed the door.

THURSDAY

Up EARLY the next morning, he was too restless to stay in his room. He dressed and went out to the street. The city was still in the hands of the Arabs at this hour. The white marble banks, the pretentious shops, shuttered and silent. He walked down beside camels shuffling, loose gaited, to the market place. Lost under immense weights, tiny burros skipped delicately, driven by urchins in skull caps.

He walked across the dusty square and took a seat outside the bar by the cinema. The coffee was thick but hot.

He drank it, dragging his mind from Arran to Caroline. He had awakened with a contrived sense of responsibility towards her. It was a charge he accepted with misgiving.

The market stirred to life. Showing no more than eyes and bare heels, Arab servants shopped, enlivening their bargaining with shrill cries of rejection. On the other side of the square, a police jeep was parked, the officers raffish behind tinted glasses. Goats straddled to be milked and in front of him, the house sparrows flapped in the thick dust.

Uneasy under the eyes of the police, he left a coin on the table and started back up the hill. Cooks was open. He went in and bought two tickets for the ferry, arranged for hotel reservations, and a car to meet him in Algeciras. Then he walked across the road to the hotel. Another police jeep was passing. He stepped into the shade of the lobby, gratefully. Caroline was at the cashier's desk, signing the last of her travellers' cheques. She saw him and came over.

Her face was relaxed as if she had woken to a day better than yesterday. She gave him the sheaf of notes without hesitation. As her hands touched his, he felt them cool again.

"I missed you," she said. A porter was stacking their bags. She walked across to tip the man.

Bain paid the bill, irritated by the need to take money from her. As he waited for change, he noted the eagerness with which she came back to the desk.

"You might at least say you're glad to see me!" She smiled, but her eyes meant exactly what she said.

That's how it would always be, he thought. Day in, day out, she'd always be reassuring herself that she was wanted. He stuffed the receipted bill into his pocket. The jacket he left unbuttoned. There were two guns now to sag on his hips. Better make their outline more difficult to see. It was still hard to meet her direct gaze. Lying with a smile, a look, was too easy. And already there'd been too much lying.

"I've got no time for romantic speeches." He pointed at the waiting car.

They jolted over the flagged jetty to the waiting ferry. A few passengers were already climbing past the white-suited stewards at the bottom of the gangway. Sharley was waiting at the police control. Seeing Bain, the guide shoved his immense body through the crowd towards them. He bent his head low enough for the oil on his scalp to be seen. Then, straightening his back, he inflated his chest like an Italian tenor.

"What pain, dear sir, lady, to see you go!" Every tooth gleaming he held out his hand. "Passports, please!"

Bain hesitated for a second. He gave the guide the documents. "You've got a broad back, Sharley," he said. "Remember there's a gun in my pocket."

The fat man wagged his head, clicking his tongue. "I am an honourable man, sir. You should have no fear." He pushed to the counter. One arm blocked the way of the passenger in front of him. "Excuse!" he said with a brilliant smile and slapped the two passports in front of the policeman.

They climbed the plank to the boat deck. The engines were turning. Gangs of Arabs wrestled with ropes, casting them off. The ropes hit the oily water, scattering floating orange peel. The ship's siren sounded twice and the craft moved astern.

Sharley stood near the end of the jetty, shading his eyes with his hand, looking up at them. "Goodbye! Goodbye!" he bellowed. Then as though he had intended the moment to have drama, he yelled: "More news! He buys a house near Malaga! Find the agent!" Waving one short arm, he trotted along beside the moving ship. "I ask nothing for this," he wailed. "Nothing! Goodbye!" He disappeared into the Customs shed.

The ship was backing into deep water. Through the ports of the first class saloon, Bain saw the Spanish women, using their fans as though their wrists turned on jewelled movements. Stiff, arrogant, the army officers slapped improbable riding boots. Down below, the Moors and the common soldiery curled on the deck, their heads wrapped against the sun. A paso doble blared from the loudspeaker.

"A house in Malaga," Caroline said softly. Her tone was as if she might destroy the building with the words. She had her arms along the deck rails, her cheek resting on them.

He put his hand under her chin, bringing up her face. She stood with legs braced against the roll of the ship, long black hair streaming in the breeze. When she smiled back at him, her momentary bitterness seemed forgotten.

"I've taken you at your word, Caroline," he said suddenly. "I've booked a room for you in Torremolinos. I'm going on to Malaga."

She nodded but her teeth caught at her bottom lip. "I told you I wanted to help, not hinder." There was little conviction in her voice. "How far is that from where you'll be?"

"About six or seven miles," he said with sufferance. "And there are telephones. I'll probably hire a Vespa. The moment *you* put a foot in Malaga, everything becomes doubly dangerous. If he saw you he'd start running." He tucked her arm under his. "I'm used to making myself inconspicuous." They walked forward and sat on coiled bleached rope. They were in open water now, meeting the cross-currents and the ship pitched more violently. Fine spray blew salt on their faces. She covered her hair with a scarf.

He eyed her sourly, irritated by the misery in her face, the droop in her shoulders. This was what she called help, he reflected. With every gesture a reproach. What the hell did she suppose they were going into! The danger of England seemed far away at that moment. Pipe-smoking cops. The colourless relentlessness of Scotland Yard with its attention to rules—even if the cops invented a few of their own as they went. Beyond the line of mountains, north of

103

the ship, the law was a cloaked figure with a patent-leather hat and a carbine. About the Guardia Civil, Bain had no illusions. In one of their barracks, there'd be no niceties of police procedure. Let them suspect guilt and they'd try to extract a confession with the butts of their rifles. One thing favoured him. Spain was a country where death occasioned little more than a hurried sign of the cross. Arran was a foreigner. Unknown and with nothing to connect him to Bain. If he were found with a bullet in his head, there'd be a great deal of correspondence with Madrid. As long as Bain kept his head, nothing more. In any case, if he could get Caroline to stay in Torremolinos, she'd be out of it all. With luck, he could even move her to Gibraltar on the pretext of meeting him there.

She touched his sleeve. "I'll go to this hotel," she said quietly. "I'm suddenly frightened, Mac. Do you know what it is to love somebody and be frightened for them?"

He wiped the salt spray from his mouth. In spite of the sun and the breeze, she conjured up a menace that he acknowledged. "There's no need to be scared," he lied. "About love . . .." he shrugged. "Why complicate things? Isn't what we have sufficient, Caroline? Do you have to tie a label to it?"

She was using the end of a finger nail to pick at the strands of hemp. "You're frightened," she accused. "Frightened of a word."

He answered, surer now what he meant to tell her. Hoping she might understand. "You're right. It's a word that terrifies me. How can I tell if I *love* you? All I know is that I want what is best for you. How strong this feeling will be when your interests conflict with mine. . . ." He hunched his shoulders.

She got up, teetering a little on narrow heels. The last two days had deepened the tan on her face. The worry lines were still whiter by contrast. She looked at him steadily. "I'll stay content with what I have," she said. "I think you're the most honest man I've ever met, Mac." She came over and put the back of her hand against his face. "I'm going below."

He was glad to be alone yet he acknowledged the effort she had made to leave him. They were more than half way across the Straits. The white mass ahead was breaking up into the sprawling town of Algeciras. To the east, Gibraltar rose like a giant black dog, squatting on its haunches.

Inevitably she had talked of the thing that he had resisted all his life. Man's nature was to resist woman. When you dragged in the word love, the fight became dirty.

He leaned over the rails, watching the small yacht that bounced astern. A boat like that—maybe you could buy one for ten thousand pounds. Life would be cheap, apart from the cost of running the craft. You could tie up in a hundred places that were no more than names, now. Cape Verde, Madagascar, Mozambique. It had been too long since he'd taken a dream and made reality of it. Almost nervously, he looked over his shoulder, as if expecting to see Caroline standing there. Sharing a dream was the hardest thing of all.

He walked aft and had a beer in the saloon. That last shout of the guide's meant, with luck, the end of the journey. It all worked out logically. Where better for Arran to collect his money than in Tangier. There were no questions, no currency controls. A couple of hours on the ferry and he was in the heart of Andalusia. All those months, the one-handed man had talked of grey-violet mountains with sombre gorges. The smell of a bull ring on fiesta day. The dignity of the Spanish people. And of their fidelity as friends. Arran had always been strong on fidelity.

There were mules visible now on the road that skirted the shore. Dust behind them and a dog running silent, tongue lolling, under the mule cart. With loud blasts of the siren, the ship rounded the end of the breakwater and fussed to the jetty.

They walked down the gangway and into the Customs sheds. Two signs hung from the roof. PASAPORTE-

ADUANA. Grouped loosely under them were twenty police. Nothing in their uniform distinguished them from those who lounged on the square beyond the barrier. Breeches, leggings, caps worn at an angle and the inevitable tinted glasses.

Bain hefted his two bags to the counter. The cop donned soiled cotton gloves and tipped the two cases on their sides. *"Donde va?"* he asked, lifting his chin.

"To Malaga," answered Bain.

The cop chalked the bags indifferently. *"Pasaporte,"* he said and flicked a finger towards the wicket at the end of the shed.

This was a high-domed man with flat black hair and a dove-grey suit. He took the landing card Bain had completed and checked it against the passport. He entered the number of the visa on a list. "How long do you stay in Spain?" The concession to a foreign language was made with difficulty. The man's eyes were inscrutable.

"A couple of weeks," answered Bain. "Perhaps more." He tried reading the visa list upside down. The entry against his name seemed the same as the rest.

"You may leave," said the official and reached for Caroline's documents.

Beyond the barriers, the jetty became a dusty square where ramshackle buses hooted their way past pavement cafés. Hotel touts, pointing at the signs on their caps, scurried from one passenger to another. Like sparrows foraging under the beaks of pigeons, small boys ducked under the touts' waving arms. "Parker Fifty-one, meester!" they called. "Best watch, contraband!" For fifty yards square, there was nothing but dirt, confusion and the smell of rotting fish.

As they came to the gate in the barrier, a chauffeur pushed his head from a parked Buick. "Wagons-Lits-Cook!" he called.

Bain opened the door. "Ellis," he said. "You know where to go?"

The driver wore a dark blue shirt, an oversize cap with an eagle above the peak. He spoke fair English, displaying a dozen gold teeth. "First to Torremolinos, señor. Then the Emperatriz in Malaga." He let in the clutch, scattering the crowd.

The road followed the curve of the bay. Tall spiked grass rose from the brackish water. A few lean cows browsed disconsolately. To the east, a road forked to Gibraltar. There was a police post at the cross. Once more the passports were inspected, the chalk marks on their baggage. On the open highway, the Spaniard pushed the Buick. He drove with one hand on the horn button, four wheels fair in the middle of the route. Occasionally a horn blared from behind. The driver blocked any attempt to overtake by menacing twists of the wheel. Other cars employing the same technique, he passed on the wrong side.

When they first entered the car, Bain had held Caroline by the hand. The lurch of the vehicle as it rode the chuckholes made contact impossible. They separated to sit silent in the corners, hanging to the arm slings. Pine forests, dark against the brilliant sunshine, red tilled earth and shimmering olive trees. Dusty villages with a few patched boats pulled up on the beach.

In the small town, the driver wheeled the Buick through jaywalking tourists, barely slackening speed. A red-faced man in shorts and a straw cap bawled abuse.

"And thy mother!" called the chauffeur, in Spanish. As if refreshed, he drove with still more abandon. "Marbella," he said over his shoulder. In English, he telescoped his consonants, lisping the sibilants. "Beautiful—with many foreigners." He controlled the wheel with his elbow, the fingers of that arm held lightly over the horn button. With the other hand, he waved at the mountainside, dark with old pines. "The Generalissimo hunts there, so they say." He bit his words to a stop as if, suddenly, they were poisoning him. He braked hurriedly.

Ahead, one each side of the road and moving slowly

towards them, were two Civil Guards. One held up his hand. He had a short-barrelled rifle slung over his shoulder, an automatic on his hip and a cloth flap that let down from his hat to protect his neck from the sun. Without haste, he bent at the open window, inspecting the interior of the car with relentless suspicion.

"*Donde va, señor?*" he asked Bain.

The driver's tone was cautious. "*Malaga,*" he cut in. "*Son dos etranjeros,*" he explained.

The Guard pushed back the brim of his patent leather hat, still searching for signs of nonconformity. Then he spat without emphasis. "*Andar!*" he instructed.

Bain watched the two figures in the driving mirror as they moved into the dust, an ominous patrol. The car had been stopped twice in sixty miles. All over Spain it would be the same. The Guardia Civil travelled the roads, trains, boats, buses. Always in pairs, sniffing out insurrection, obeying none but their superior.

"Very strong, the Guardia." The driver sucked his teeth, managing to make the sound derisory. "When *he* comes to hunt, every centimetre of the forest is controlled. Regiments are in trees and for a week we are told he is in the north. By God, he is three people to be in so many places at one time. The saviour of Spain!" he said loudly and started humming flamencos, using his nose like a flute.

They climbed the long slope into Torremolinos. Past the bank built like a ship and the hideous villas down to the beach. Through a square lined with pepper trees. "Torremolinos," said the driver. As if cheered, he added: "Malaga, twelve kilometers."

Bain felt Caroline move closer. He put his arm round her shoulder. Where a eucalyptus grove made the air pungent, the car lurched suddenly to the left. They climbed a driveway for fifty yards and stopped in front of a stone building.

The driver swivelled in his seat, taking off his dark glasses and smiling brilliantly. "Hotel el Pinar!" he said.

The hotel graced the mountainside. Rough stone, doors of old wood studded with bosses, the place had been built with care and vision. A belt of pines sheltered it from the north. A boy took Caroline's bags. They went after him, into the cool interior. A dozen monasteries had been ransacked to furnish the fumed panelling, the tapestry on the wall, the brilliant tiles. Now that the time had come, Bain wanted to stay. He went upstairs with Caroline. In her bedroom, she stood at the mirror, wiping the dust from her face with cotton.

He opened the window, looking beyond the twisted iron to pink-flowering shrubs round a fountain. On the horizon, the peaks were jagged, like teeth on a hound's jaw. He turned suddenly, the knot of pity bitter in his throat.

"Caroline!" he began. When she faced him, his courage went and his words stumbled. "I wanted you to know— what I said was true, about me wanting the best for you."

She was brushing her hair, tilting her head so that the long black sweep swung clear of her face. "What was in that letter you wrote to me? The one I never got?" she asked quietly.

"Only the truth," he said obstinately. "About your husband."

She continued to brush till the hair was smooth, like the skin of a ripe plum. "Do you know how I'm feeling at this moment?" she asked. "Knowing you will be leaving this room and that I might never see you again?"

He put out a hand, patting her shoulder mechanically. "That's crazy." Anger was better than watching the misery in her face and he made his voice rough. "If that's all the faith you've got in me!"

She took his lapels, shaking them, emphasising her words. "I've got faith," she told him. "But I know what Peter's capable of. You saw those men today. The police on the road. They're cruel, Mac, and stupid. Peter can handle people like that without them knowing it. He could do the same to you here as he did in England. And I'd never know what happened to you."

He sensed what was coming and tried to stop it. "*I know* Arran. I know every lousy trick he's capable of pulling." He held her at arm's length. "Listen to me. I rarely make promises but here's one. When this is over, you'll never have cause to worry about me."

Her mouth was drawn with the effort of smiling. "Once you told me you didn't like lectures. But keeping out of trouble is as much a matter of common sense as morals."

He hunched his shoulders. "Getting even with Arran hasn't anything to do with either. If I left him to God's will, he'd be sitting on my tombstone, laughing his head off." If he could, he would have hidden his head in her lap, freed of an idea he could no longer control. But it was too late.

"I want you safe, nothing more," she said obstinately. "God knows that's reasonable enough. For the first time in my life, I feel that I am wanted. That matters to a woman, Mac."

The longer he postponed going, the harder it would be. He smiled an assurance he could only hope for, forcing his voice to be casual. "I'll ring you in the morning," he promised. "You get a good night's rest." He lowered his head to kiss her but she broke away. She faced the mirror, brushing her hair vigorously, as though it were of great importance to her. As Bain went to the door, he saw that her shoulders were shaking.

He shut the door behind him. More and more, he was fearing the compulsive pity she provoked in him. These past few days, there'd been a dozen times when he had found himself equating her interests with his. Almost imperceptibly, his objectives had changed. He had started out to find Arran—to get his share of the loot. The idea of killing had been a last resort. Now, he knew that he wanted all the loot *and* Arran's death. The change, he told himself, was because of Caroline. Resenting her influence over him, he went out to the car and shut her from his mind.

He scouted the countryside as a man will when the lie of a copse, the bend in a road, can mean his safety. Once past the military airfield, the suburbs of Malaga were a struggle of mean boxlike dwellings, warehouses, factories. The cobbled highway accepted the traffic without discrimination. Street cars, automobiles, mule carts, cyclists. All moved at capacity speed, avoiding the pedestrians who turned with blind faith into the stream.

A bridge spanned a dry river bed and they were in an avenue of lime trees. Knots of police stood in the shade watching the ice-cream vendors, the priests who strolled, telling their beads.

"Avenida Generalissimo Franco," the driver said into the mirror. He rolled the syllables sonorously and spat into the breeze. Now that he was in his home city, he was more talkative. Left was Larios where lay the great shops. The Post Office building. Police Headquarters. The Buick left the shade of the limes and turned past the pink bullring with its tall incinerator tower. Here, the neighbourhood acquired tone. Villas nudged one another up the hill to Gibralfaro. On the right, a large hotel was half hidden behind tattered date palms.

"Hotel Miramar," said the driver with respect.

Bain's hotel was a mile away, on the same street. He paid the driver and went into the Emperatriz. On the way up to his room, he took a map of the city. Outside his window, a single line railroad rattled east to Velez. To the west, to the city and Torremolinos. Thirty yards away, the sea washed grey sand.

He put his head out the window, leaning over the flower beds below. It was an easy drop. If he had to get in and out this room, unobserved, the trellis work under the bougainvillæa would hold his weight. Three inches below the sill, the blossom was thick. He put his hand in to the wrist, tugging the rough stem. It was at least an inch in diameter.

The keys, the gun he had taken from Caroline, he rolled in a plastic sponge bag. He attached this to the vine, covering it with blossom and leaves. The second gun, he hung from his inner left jacket pocket, with safety pins. It made no bulge and was easy to reach. Then he washed his hands clean and went downstairs.

At the back of the hotel, flagged paths circled a swimming-pool to an iron gate in the high wall. He unlocked it. Outside, a beaten dirt track flanked the railroad ties. He followed it towards the city, closing his nostrils against the stench from the filth in the spear grass. On the beach, crude shacks still gave shelter to the people who lived there. Goats, tethered from front to hind leg, browsed in the open garbage pits. Naked below the navel, tiny children stoned the curs that scavenged. The dogs ran snarling, their tails bent between their legs.

On the right, the mass of the Miramar Hotel rose, above palms white with dust. Sweat was collecting under Bain's arm, pouring down his sides. He took off his jacket, balancing the weight of the gun in the crook of his arm. He sat on one of the square stone blocks that littered the foreshore and lit a cigarette. The walls round the Miramar were high but gapped. They offered no obstacle and there was cover right to the rear doors of the hotel. None the less, this was no place to kill Arran. He'd need a key to the man's door. Making it took time—to fit it, still longer. The chance of doing all that, unobserved, was one in a hundred.

He put on a pair of dark glasses and climbed one of the streets at the side of the bullring. Avoiding the main thoroughfares, he worked his way up to the Cathedral. Here, steps went down to a bar. He sat in the cool, by great brass-bound vats of wine, and ordered a brandy. Three men were throwing for drinks at the bar, intent on the dice in the leather cup. Nobody paid attention to Bain.

In this dark cellar, out of the glare of the street, he felt safe. A hundred times, since he'd walked out of Gerald Road Police Station, he had lived the scene about to be played. Usually, he waited in a darkened room, behind a curtain, savouring the terror in his partner's face. Then he pulled the trigger, pumping shells into a body that no longer moved. Sometimes, it was a car on a lonely road. Or a shadowed garden where he stood flat against a tree. But always, there was the gun in his hand and in Arran's eyes —terror.

He draped his jacket across his knees, splashing the brandy with soda from a tired siphon. He drank slowly, considering the best way of finding Arran's room number. It had to be done carefully. None of the expertise gathered these past ten years would be of use.

He left a coin for the drink and walked down to the Telephone Building. At the desk, he bought a couple of slugs from the girl and took a vacant wall phone. He dialled the Miramar Hotel. Hunching his back to hide the manœuvre, he draped a folded handkerchief over the mouthpiece.

"Hotel Miramar! *Dega me!*" said the voice the other end of the line.

"Let me talk to someone in English," Bain said.

There was a pause then a second voice cut in, suave and in English. "Hotel Miramar, sir. Are you wanting something?"

He leaned into the mouthpiece, smiling sincerity. "I'm trying to get in touch with someone who arrived from Tangier yesterday. A Mr Farran." He spelled the word carefully.

"Just one little minute, sir," said the clerk. "I shall see." In a moment, he continued. "We have no one of that name, sir."

Bain spoke with decision. "That seems unlikely. I have the address in front of me. Miramar Hotel, Malaga. Will you look again?"

"I have looked, sir." The man was equally definite. "You are sure it is *Farran?* We had a Mr *Arran* but that gentleman left this morning."

"No!" Bain left no doubt. "That's not my man. Thanks for your help, anyway. It's just possible that I have the wrong information." He used the handkerchief on the mouthpiece to wipe his neck.

He went back to the cellar bar and drank two more brandies. Slowly and with growing confidence. Sometimes, it happened that certainty bucked all laws of probability. Guiding your fingers to pick just one card from a full deck. Steadying your nerves when your horse ran fifth along the back stretch. And now he knew that he was very close to Arran.

So confident was he that he took off the dark glasses and walked down to the Telephone Building, taking the breeze in his face. He used the same phone to dial the same number. The second voice was painstakingly courteous.

"Hotel Miramar, sir. Are you wanting something?"

Bain faked an English accent, clipping his words, making them peremptory. "This is the office of the British Consul. We have a telegram here for Mr Peter Arran. Will you please connect me with his room."

There was no suspicion in the man's voice, only deference. "I regret, señor. Señor Arran left the hotel this morning."

Bain made a sound like a short tempered official. "Then you'd better give me his address if you have it." He waited, pencil poised over paper, smiling as the man replied.

"We have here, señor, this address. Finca San Carlos, Rincon de la Victoria, Malaga."

It was a good place to think, the cool cellar. He took his time with yet another weak brandy, considering the next step. Rincon de la Victoria was a village unmarked on the map he had taken. He could risk no inquiries at the hotel. There must be as few links as possible between the man at the Emperatriz and the one who went to the finca. There was a phone book in the bar and he took it. The local office of the Spanish automobile association was listed on a street nearby. He found his way there. It was an old house. A stairway circled the interior courtyard. A girl in the office spoke English and he tried another role.

"My wife and I are staying in the city. We're looking for drives we could make in the area. Maybe you'd let me look at a few large-scale maps?"

The girl brought half a dozen folders. He carried them to a table, spreading them and using pencil and paper as if preparing an itinerary. A couple of times, he asked the girl about points of interest to the north, to the west. Rincon de la Victoria, he found a dozen kilometres east of the city. On the map, a thin black line pointed up from the village, skirting the valley. It corkscrewed north, disappearing where lightly sketched fins showed mountains several thousand feet high. For the first few miles of the road, black dots clustered each side of it.

He took one of the other maps to the girl at the desk. "These black dots," he asked. "Are they villages, hamlets or what?"

She shook her head. "Fincas, estancias, señor." She searched for the words. "Farms—what you would call ranches in America."

"Then I think we'll stick to the coast." He grinned. "The roads are better."

She carried the maps back to their place. "Torremolinos attracts many foreigners," she said. She shut the door of the cupboard as if on all foreigners.

At a shop on Larios, he bought a cheap pair of field-glasses and a book, in Spanish, on ornithology. There were thirty coloured plates of strange-looking birds. He intended carrying no passport when he went to see Arran. The Civil Guards were to be avoided. If he were to run into a patrol, memory of an idiot foreigner, bird-watching, was an innocuous one to leave. There was an accessory shop behind the market. There he bought mechanic's overalls and an outsize pair of motoring goggles. All he needed now was the means to get him to Arran's farmhouse. And, with luck, back again. A bicycle would do but goggles on a bicycle struck a dangerous note of incongruity. A car was cumbersome. A scooter ideal. It could climb the side of a mountain. You could hide it in long grass. And the roads were covered with them.

He rambled through the network of lanes between the great avenue and the market. Scanning the signs over the garages, he found one that said:

Motos Alquilar Garage Muñoz

He went in. A dozen battered scooters were parked in a wooden rack. Flat in the oily dirt, a man was tinkering with the rear end of an ancient Citroën. Hearing Bain, he rolled over, propping himself with the mallet in his hand.

"*Buenos dias, señor! Que quiere?*"

Bain used pantomime and his phrase book to explain what he wanted. The Spaniard climbed to his feet, wiping grease from his face with a filthier rag.

"All are superb machines!" He waved a hand at the rack. "Some are still better than others. For how long, señor?"

"Three days," said Bain.

"Three days!" The garage proprietor tried to hide his pleasure. He lifted a scooter from the rack, bouncing it on its wheels, flicking the rusting chrome. "Here is a magnificent *moto*. For three days, I am willing to make a concession. Six hundred pesetas." He dabbed his nose, using the rag as a screen from behind which he watched Bain's reaction. "*Por Dios!*" he said suddenly. "And I make you a gift of the gasolene!"

Bain tried the controls. The price the man asked for the scooter's hire was high. But the brakes worked and the tiny motor buzzed like an angry hornet. He gave the man six hundred peseta bills.

"And the señor's address?" The man was at his desk. Head at an angle, he wrote in flowery style on a billhead.

"Williams," said Bain, choosing a name incomprehensible to a Spaniard. "Care of the British Consulate, Torremolinos."

Too arrogant to ask, the man wrote an approximation of the name Bain had told him. "You have papers, señor. Some means of identification?"

"With me, no," Bain said pleasantly. "If you insist, I will fetch them."

The man blotted the receipt hurriedly. "It is not I who insist but the police. If I am asked, I shall say you are bringing your papers. If not . . ." He shrugged and filled the small tank with gas. Slapping the saddle, he smiled at Bain. "Pleasant distractions, señor."

There was a satchel behind the saddle. Bain stuffed it with the things he had bought. On front and back mudguard, two enamel plates proclaimed the scooter the property of Garage Muñoz. He chugged the vehicle back to the hotel, trying its manœuvrability. It turned in its own length. At a pinch, it would go in the back of a car and the speedometer showed fifty miles an hour. He took one of the streets at the side of the Emperatriz and rode to the waterfront. Over the dirt path to the iron gate in the wall behind the garden. There were a few people splashing in the pool, fifty yards away. The sun was low, but still hot. Only the shutters in his room were open. He pushed the gate. Inside, sheets were bleaching on a line. He used them as cover to wheel the scooter to an outhouse. He kicked the door open. Cement sacks and scaffolding were piled against the walls. He dragged the scooter to the end, out of sight. A small kit of tools bulged under the pillion seat. He took off the two plates advertising the garage. He broke a bolt on each to justify himself in case of inquiry. Then he left the articles he had bought beside the scooter and went into the hotel.

He ate late, choosing a seat at a window where he could watch the shed. Women collected the sheets but the door to the shed remained closed.

FRIDAY

In the morning, he woke to the rattle of the first train outside. He stood at the window, watching it pass. It was an ancient locomotive leaking steam and hauling three small coaches. The windows were open. In the first coach, four Civil Guards sat upright, as though even the empty morning were worthy of suspicion. There was a haze over the sea and the lizards ran on the wall in the early sun. He dressed in slacks and a shirt and took the loaded automatic in his pocket. Downstairs, a sleepy waiter gave him breakfast. The garden was empty. He opened the shed and wheeled out the scooter, unseen.

At a bar a mile east, he stopped for a second coffee. Then he used the phone to call Torremolinos. Caroline answered.

"I found our friend," he said carefully. "I may go there for lunch or for dinner. I want you to stay right where you are. I'll call you later tonight."

Her answer was almost as guarded as his. "Be careful of the traffic," she told him. "I'll be waiting for you to telephone. I love you," she added quickly and hung up.

There was a grocer's store next door. He bought fruit, bread and cheese. A bottle of mineral water. Then he went east again. A hard-topped road followed the coastline. He rode past fishing nets spread in the sun to dry, a hundred yards long. Past beach shacks like child's square bricks. Black holes in the rocky outcrops where the railroad tracks vanished. Five miles out of the city, a long slope straggled up to a dry plain littered with boulders. He dismounted and pulled the scooter into the lee of some scrub olives. He changed his clothes quickly, batting the horse-flies from his neck, the ants that dropped from the grey dead boughs overhead. He made a bundle of slacks and shirt and stowed it in the saddle bag. The stiff overalls scratched his skin.

They were hot. He undid the top buttons, letting in what air there was. Then he used a roll of adhesive to tape the gun to the underside of a foot rest. The goggles bothered him. Their padded frames touched his cheek bones, his forehead, giving him the sense of eye sockets five times too big. But the thick mica hid a great part of his face.

A mile ahead, a deserted tower marked a bend in the highway. It had showed on the map as the entrance to Rincon de la Victoria. He put the scooter down the hill. Over a bridge where the words VIVA FRANCO were stencilled on the cement props, into the village. It was a thin straggling hamlet with length but no breadth. Outside the Civil Guard office, a man sat in a chair, reading a paper in the sun. As Bain passed, the officer looked up indifferently. A door in a house opened, gapping the whitewash like a bad tooth. A woman pitched a pail of dirty water to the street. A few dogs set up a forlorn gallop behind the scooter but in Rincon de la Victoria nothing else moved. In front of some new villas at the end of the village, mulberry trees gave shade. He pulled the scooter under them and sat watching the summit of the dusty track that spiralled away from him. Thirty yards ahead, an old coastal fort had been turned into a Civil Guard Barrack. It would be from here that the night patrols set out. Always in pairs, wrapped in grey-green cloaks, searching the seashore, the mountains.

A mule caravan was coming from the opposite direction. Dust from the animals' hooves hid the front of the barracks. Bain used the moment to kick the scooter into action and headed it into the mountains. He climbed the left side of the valley. To the east, the ground sloped down to a dry river bed where bushes with brilliant coloured blooms pushed among the stones. Between vines and olives growing at fantastic angles, deep gullies cut down to join the river bed. One silent cyclist, a peasant asleep behind a mule, were the only people he saw in six miles. Five or six farms showed on the slopes. None bore the name San Carlos. His sleeves were soaked and his wrists blue where the dye in the material had run. The scooter stuttered loudly in the thinner air. Whenever the road dipped, he cut the motor. Suddenly the sign was there in front of him. As he had known it must be. A shingle on the end of an olive pole, painted in faded green. FINCA SAN CARLOS. There was nothing else.

Where the shingle pointed, a second track dropped precipitously. He pushed the scooter down the grade. So deep was the track here that the rocky soil was over his head. It was a natural gully with ballast added to give the surface traction. He got on the saddle again, free-wheeling. At each curve in the gully, he stopped and scouted the way ahead. After a mile, he came to a brake where cane grew to the edge of the track. Beyond, the track disappeared into a thick belt of pine. Near the road, the canes leaned drunkenly. Sun and wind had bared their roots. The earth that belonged there powdered the road surface. Fresh in the soft dirt, were sharp car tracks.

He shoved the scooter into the cane brake and laid it on its side. It took a screwdriver to get the gun free of its tape wrapping. He put food, water and the field-glasses in a paper sack and started through the cane towards the trees. Clouds of midges rose under his feet, clogging his mouth and his nostrils. The saw-edged leaves whipped at his hands, his bare ankles, bringing blood. He turned backwards, using his shoulders to force the cane apart, covering his mouth with a handkerchief. When he reached the trees, he lay for a while on the thick pine needles. Then he rinsed his mouth with mineral water and crawled to the edge of the track. Under the sun its dusty length was a white ribbon between the pines. A quarter mile ahead was another clearing. He put the glasses on it, cupping his hands over the lens to avoid tell-tale reflection. The cheap binoculars were not powerful enough to bring detail in sharp focus. But he could see the long white farmhouse, red-roofed, a truck parked in front of it. Figures moved at the back of the vehicle. He went twenty feet deeper into the plantation. Propping himself against a tree, he ate his food.

The sound of the truck motor came clear. He went down on his stomach again, elbows square in the pine needles, training the glasses on the clearing. The truck turned then roared up the track towards him. He lay where he was, still, as it passed. There were two men in the cab. At it took the bend, he had a brief vision of empty crates in the back, a litter of straw. The food that remained, he kept. It might be a long time before he had the chance to eat again. Then he started to work his way through the woods, keeping the sun on his left. There were no birds to rise squawking in sudden alarm. He saw nothing that lived but the tree spiders.

After a while, he tired of brushing their sticky webs from his face. For twenty minutes, he walked like that. Every sense alert, straining his nerves for the unexpected. The only sound was the faint crunch his own feet made.

Near at hand, he heard women's voices. He stopped then moved on cautiously, checking every few yards. Still again, he went down flat, wriggling like a snake. The pines grew thinner here. The sun struck through the boughs, patterning the ground around him with shadow. The clearing was thirty yards away. He crawled nearer, wiping the salt sweat from his eyes. Back, legs, itched in a hundred places. But he kept even his breathing shallow in the attempt to remain hidden.

The walls of the house were white and thick, broken with deep shadow where open shutters swung a little in the wind. Fifty yards away were the servants' quarters—a cement block building with a flat roof where washing hung. There was a ladder against the smaller house. One girl stood on it, slapping lime on the wall. A second woman held the ladder. Their voices were shrill and clear. He got to his feet and moved round to the front of the house.

A great pepper tree stood before the front door. There was a patch of grass, green under a hose. Flower beds in front of the windows blazed red and crimson. Beyond them, in the full glare of the fierce sun, Arran lay on a rubber mattress. He was stripped to a slip, his face turned upwards, both arms outstretched in the position of a man crucified.

Instinctively, Bain's fingers found the butt of the automatic. He tensed—as if sure the other must smell his presence. Arran's eyes stayed shut. With infinite care, Bain started to haul his weight up the bole of a tree. Fifteen feet above, a thick branch pointed at the house, like an outstretched finger. He straddled it, his back against the trunk of the tree. He was thirty yards away from the still figure.

As he watched, a woman came from the house. She was young, high-breasted and wore her straight yellow hair in a pony tail. She stopped in the doorway, scanning the clearing. Then she called to the man on the rubber mattress.

"I meant exactly what I said, you know, Peter. One night's quite enough for me in a half-furnished barn."

Arran's eyes were still closed. He made no reply. She ran to him, her face sullen against the sun, her mouth petulant. "Do you hear!" she screamed. "I'm going back to Malaga until you make this place civilised." She stood over Arran, shouting down, "Do you *hear* me?" she repeated.

Arran's left hand grabbed her ankle. He pulled her to the ground beside him. Then he cut at her cheeks with the palm of his hand. Twice, jolting her head first left then right. "Shout at me just once again," he said savagely, "and you do go, but for good." He sat up, smiling.

She crouched where she had fallen, holding her cheeks. "You hurt me!" she sounded bewildered. Tears came with the words and she hid her face in her arms.

Arran watched her for a second before getting to his feet. "Get up!" he ordered. He prodded her with bare toes. "And get your bags packed. You're going into Malaga, Elizabeth."

The tone of his voice stopped the heave in her shoulders. She pawed at his arm, her face ugly with tears. "You're not going to leave me there, Peter? I've got no money. You *can't* leave me. I'll . . ."

"You'll *what?*" asked Arran quietly. He touched his toffee grey hair delicately then pushed the girl towards the house. "*I'll* tell you what you're going to do! You're going to catch the next plane back to London." He walked behind her, his stump prodding her back, pointing his words. "You filthy little peasant!"

Bain dug his nails into the rough bark, leaning out in an attempt to see them into the house. There was no sound from inside for a quarter hour. Then the girl came to the dark doorway, carrying two cases. A new convertible rolled out of the barn. Arran backed it precisely, waiting till the girl lifted her bags into the car. He had put on a canary-coloured shirt. A white silk scarf was knotted inside the collar.

The sound of the motor brought the maids round to the front of the house. They stood hand in hand, watching Arran like two scared animals. He called over to them in Spanish.

"*Adiós*, Paquita! *Adiós*, Isabellita!" His mouth was gentle and he waved an arm. "Tell the señora to go with God! She returns no more."

They waved back, using the soft dialect, two obedient children. "*Vaya con Dios, señora! Vaya con Dios!*"

The car wheeled and accelerated up the drive between the pines. Pebbles scattered and dust hung in the air. When it had settled, the two girls walked back to their quarters. Whispering as if frightened their words might be overheard.

Bain looked at his watch. It was three o'clock. The hour of the siesta. The house stood empty, the dark open door an invitation. The maids would sleep. He dropped to the ground, careless now about noise. Once he was in the house he could see the maids' quarters from one of the back windows. He ran through the trees and out to the clearing. In the shade of the pepper tree, he stopped. The weathered door was wide, revealing walls two feet thick. He could see a tiled floor, littered with shavings. The load the truck had brought had been left in the hall. Chests with iron handles. A refrigerator. Carved head-pieces for beds. Beyond the litter of furniture, a wide staircase was dark against the white walls.

He counted the windows. There were eight above and eight below. Bent iron made graceful grilles in front of each. At night, the heavy door would be shut. The giant key turned, the bolts rammed home. Whatever Arran had to protect would be as safe as if in a bank. He thought back, remembering Arran's face when they had found jewellery stuffed in a flour bin—pinned to the outside of second story curtains. Always there had been the amused smile, thickened by the scar, as Arran pointed his stump in triumph. "Only whores or nouveau riche would think of a place like that," he said happily. "Know your woman and you'll know where her jewellery can be found."

Arran's money would be in no bank. And a gun in his neck would make him say where. Bain squatted in the lee of the tree trunk. The certainty he had in Malaga was justified. Arran would sleep in the house alone tonight. A pillow over the muzzle of the automatic and the maids would hear nothing. Dead, Arran posed no problem. There were a dozen places on the way up from Rincon de la Victoria where a body might be hidden. Overhangs in the mountain side where one stone prised free would bring down an avalanche. The maids would scarcely miss a master they had known one day. They were good for a week or more. Two Spanish females who would question Arran's absence only when their food ran out. Even the scooter could be hidden in the car if the top were up. The car itself could be left in the park in front of the Miramar, one last source of confusion.

There in the shade of the tree, the scent of the massed flowers was heavy. High overhead, a buzzard wheeled lazily, black against the blue sky. He got to his feet, shaking his head. A little more and he'd be asleep. There was no time to spare. Arran could make the round trip to Malaga in a half hour in the Jaguar. Before that, Bain had to be sure he could enter the house after nightfall.

He crossed the green. At the open door, he took off his shoes. Tying the laces in knots, he hung the shoes round his neck. At the far end of the hall, sun shone through a rear window. There were flies buzzing in the shaft of light and a clock ticked in a room to his left. The grilles on the windows were old. The screws that held them, lost in rust and paint. Entry through a window was impossible without a hacksaw. There must be another door at the back for the maids. If it proved as impractical to force as the one at the front of the house, he had no choice. He would have to stow away in one of the rooms. At the back, all the windows were shuttered save the one in the hall. He felt his way along the dark corridor till his fingers met wood. He groped for the door handle and turned it.

He was in a large kitchen with a flagged floor. The walls were bright with copper pans and the door to the back yard was open. A Spaniard sat in a chair in front of the charcoal stove, fanning the flame under a coffee pot. He came to his feet quickly yet easily, dropping the palm leaf. His chin was stiff with a week's black beard. As he challenged Bain, the man's chin lifted slightly.

"What do you want here, man?" he asked in Spanish.

Bain stood where he was, still holding the door handle. The shoes round his neck swung slightly on the tied laces. Goggles were pushed up over his forehead and the filthy overalls bulged with food and the gun.

He searched for words that would get him out of there, allay the suspicion that brightened the Spaniard's eyes. "Water," he croaked. "I want water, señor!"

"How do you come here?" The man's hand went in his pocket. He flicked a catch on the knife, springing a six-inch blade from the haft. Without haste, he sliced a piece of hard sausage. He guided it into his mouth with blade and thumb, his eyes never leaving Bain.

"By foot," Bain answered. "My *moto* is on the road above where I fell. I thought that here I might find water to drink." He pointed down at his feet. The sawing cane had cut his ankles, crusting the skin with dried blood. "And to wash," he said.

The man took a dipper of water and passed it to Bain. "Drink!" he said. "In the yard there is water to wash."

The men were close now and Bain smelt the garlic on the other's breath. Turning his back, he walked to the door. As he moved, he pulled back his shoulders to cushion the blade that must fall there.

"You are German?" said the Spaniard. It was an inquiry not an accusation.

"I am German," replied Bain.

There was a pump house in the yard. A motor worked, sending icy water along a stone channel to a basin where the women did their washing. He sat on the edge of the basin, letting the cold numb the pain from his cuts. His feet were dry in the hot sun when he reached the back door again.

"Adiós!" he called. "And many thanks!"

"Go with God," the man answered mechanically and cut into his sausage.

Bain walked up the track through the pines. Somehow, he resisted looking round at the house. Every window would be a vantage point from which eyes watched. Once beyond the first bend, he ran to the shelter of the trees. This last fifteen minutes had changed everything. Now he *had* to break into the house. It meant going to the village for hacksaw blades. If the man in the kitchen told Arran of a visitor, it could mean little. As far as Arran was concerned, Bain was safe in Brixton Prison. A stray German tourist might offend the one-handed man's sense of privacy, nothing more.

He could see light through the trees where the cane

brake started. He worked his way round till he found the gap he had forced. He pushed the scooter back on the track and hid the gun under a stone. Then he jolted back up the gully, following the fresh tyre marks left by the Jaguar. The tiny tread of the scooter tyres was lost in the deeper markings.

At the fork to the coastal road, he went into a store. The interior was heady with brandy and onion. Ants crawled thick on the olive oil containers. Dried fish glistened with salt while overhead sausage strings swung next to ancient flypapers. A sleepy-eyed man took Bain's pantomime gravely, following each gesture with interest. First he produced a comb—then a flyspray. Finally, with a smile of triumph, a package of hacksaw blades, the wrappings blotched with age.

Three miles from the village, the mountain pushed boulders to the edge of the track. Shaped like a wedge, one great stone perched on another. Smaller rocks crowded behind, spilling round the edges of the poised boulder. Bain sat there, polishing the rust from the blades with motor oil. There'd be a crowbar—a two-by-four—at the farmhouse. One end under that poised rock and a hundred tons of granite would cover the coarse yellow grass, the few wild vines beneath. The peasant who passed every day would notice no more than a fall in the rock. But it would be Arran's grave.

The sun was red over Malaga. Still he lay flat on the rock, his glasses trained on the fork in the road. Then the whine of the climbing Jaguar came clear. Bain slid from the boulder. Tyres screeched as Arran wheeled the convertible round the bend. He was alone in the car. Two hours more before it was dark. Only then could Bain go to the farmhouse. He mounted the scooter and started up to the next village. He stood in a whitewashed bar and telephoned Torremolinos. There was a faded poster in front of him. He waited for the call to come through, he read the names of toreros long since horned or retired.

When Caroline answered, he talked quickly, blocking her protest. "Listen carefully. I've no time to explain. Just do as I tell you. Pay your bill now and get out of that hotel tonight. Hire a car to take you to Gib. Wait for me at the Rock Hotel." There was no answer. "Caroline!" he said.

Her voice was small so that he could hardly catch the words. "I'm not going to do it," she whispered.

"Then I'm sunk," he said. The end was too near now. If he failed, there must be no chance of her failing with him.

She was controlling her voice with difficulty. "I knew——" she started. "Where are you, Mac?" she demanded. "I'm going to come over there, straight away."

"You're crazy!" he said sharply. "I've just seen him," he lied. "God knows how, but he's heard that you're here. I've told him no. But if he finds out, it's the end of everything I've worked for. You've got to *do* this for me, Caroline," he pleaded.

She had all the grief and weariness of a very old woman. "All right, Mac, I'll do it." She went over his instructions again. "I pay my bill and get a car to take me to Gibraltar. Then I wait at the Rock Hotel." Her voice broke. "Oh, *Mac*!" she said desperately.

"I love you," he said steadily. In that moment, he believed it. "I'll be in Gib tomorrow night. If I'm not, remember that—I love you, Caroline."

He hooked the phone to the wall and paid at the bar for the call. For a while, he stared at the dirt-streaked face in the mirror as if it belonged to a stranger. Then he went out. Lamps had come on in the village street. Tiny points of light flickered across on the mountain sides. It was cold, suddenly, and he buttoned his overalls to the neck. He would have stayed there if he could. The tiny bar rattled with dominoes, tinny music came from the cheap radio. It was warm and friendly. He got in the saddle and started down the stony track.

He cut lights and motor at the farmhouse sign and free-wheeled down the gully. The cane brake was white against the dark belt of trees. When he had pushed the scooter into shelter, he retrieved his gun from under the stone. The wind was fresher, whipping the tops of the cane, moving the boughs of the trees. He walked on the edge of the track, leaving no footprints on the weed-grown stones. He carried the gun in his hand, thumb on the safety catch.

At the edge of the clearing, he stopped. The farmhouse was in darkness—the pump motor silent. On the flat annex roof, the washing swung slowly. He circled the verge of the grass, cautiously. The window he had chosen was at the far end of the house, away from the kitchen. He stood for a moment, peering through the gap in the shutter. Something moved. He relaxed, recognising his own dim reflection in the glass. He put the gun in his pocket.

The ends of the first blade were wrapped in oily rags. He poked it through the shutters, lifting the hook from its eye. Then holding the blade with both hands, he went to work on the first bar. Steel bit into paint, then iron, the noise lost in the creak of the shutter. He used his weight, bearing down on the muffled blade. A tooth broke and the blade dragged till it snapped. He put the fragments back in the package and chose another. The iron parted suddenly. He stopped sawing to listen. He needed to make two cuts, one above the other, severing the ends of the cross bars. A slow steady pull and the grille would bend outwards. A shoulder against the window and he was in the empty room. He went to work on the second bar.

A shutter was thrown open on the second floor. With the force of the thrust it slammed against the wall. A patch of light shone from window to garden. Another shutter clattered and the light on the flower beds grew. He ran, bent double, for the trees. Then he fell, facing the house. Upstairs, downstairs, one after another the windows were thrown open. Every light in the house blazed. The only shadow left outside was under the pepper tree.

Arran stood in front of one of the upstairs windows. He

called above the sound of the wind. "Bain! *Bain!*" His voice sounded as if he was shouting through cupped hands. "Don't waste your time creeping about out there, I know you're there!"

Bolts rattled down below, the key was turned in the door and it swung inward. Bain lay still. His heart banged as though it might lift his chest from the ground. His arms were pushed out in front of him and his hands shook violently. The maid's quarters showed no sign of life. Arran had not reappeared. But the front door stood wide as if for a long-awaited guest. . . .

He worked his hand down to his pocket, found the gun and released the safety catch. Then he crawled to the blank end of the farmhouse. Deep shadow extended from the wall to the tree. He ducked into it and crouched against the stone. Ten feet to his right, shadow met light in a line as straight as a rod. He went flat again, his head inches from the ground, and snaked round the corner. He was under the first window, crawling towards the front door at a right angle. He climbed up, using his knees like a camel. He held his left hand out in guard, the gun in his right hugged close to his stomach.

The door was a foot away. Over the threshold, a long shadow stretched across the tiles. It changed shape as he watched. He ran through the opening and stopped dead.

Arran was facing the door, leaning against the refrigerator. "You've been a long time," he said quietly. "Shut the door!" His right arm was thrust deep in his trouser pocket. He moved his shoulder slightly.

"Keep it just like that!" warned Bain quickly. He backed to the door and kicked it shut.

Arran pulled his maimed arm from his pocket. Shaking his head, his smile lopsided, he let his arm drop. Bain came nearer, searching the other man's face for the fear that had to be there. Arran's pale eyes were undisturbed.

Bain wet his mouth. "You know why I'm here." The

words were cheap—like the balloon from the mouth of a cartoon desperado. He lifted the gun to give them dignity.

The thin smile stayed on Arran's face, he raised his chin slightly. Hate tightened Bain's finger on the trigger. Without thinking, he stepped back and fired, aiming over Arran's shoulder. Glass splintered with the report. Acrid smoke trickled from the barrel of the gun. Bain raised it a second time.

"I'm going to kill you," he said unsteadily.

Arran moved for the first time, loosening the scarf at his neck. He wrinkled his nose against the powder fumes, coughing. "Not now, you aren't," he gasped. He used a handkerchief to wipe his mouth. "You bloody fool! Taking me out quietly on the end of a gun seemed easy, I suppose. But you needed a frightened man. Look at me, Mac!" He smiled again, lifting both arms in the air. "Am I frightened?"

Bain stood irresolute. The urge to destroy was there but this was the wrong weapon. Arran's indifference to death was no bluff. These last seconds had shown him ready to accept it, grinning. As if his mocking certainty carried him beyond anything others might inflict on him. Suddenly Bain understood the man cared for little, even living. It would be like shooting a man already dead.

Doors banged at the back of the house. He heard steps on the flagged kitchen, the noise of people running in the corridor.

"Give me the gun quickly," said Arran.

There had been too many moments like this. Bain's obedience was automatic. He pushed the pistol into Arran's hand. The door to the hall burst open. Behind the Spanish manservant, the two maids peeped curiously, their eyes alive with excitement. The man stood for a second, a bull ready to charge. His look missed nothing in the room. He spoke to Arran in Spanish.

"There was a shot, señor. We feared an accident." He moved the glass from the broken window with a tentative

131

toe. Then he gave a quick instruction to the maids. They dragged the splinters to a corner with their feet.

Arran put the pistol on top of the refrigerator. "An accident, Pablo," he smiled. He pointed at Bain. "The German gentleman is a friend. I was explaining the mechanism of the pistol."

The man's teeth were white in his black beard. "Then good night, gentlemen." He looked directly at Bain. "*Adiós, señor*. May your feet heal rapidly."

Once they were gone, Arran nodded at the gun. "Put it back in your pocket." His voice was faintly pleased. Like that of a chess player who has heard 'check' twenty times and now says 'mate'. "For Christ's sake, sit down. This isn't a scene from the Lone Star Ranger."

They sat facing one another. Outside, the shutters were still banging in the wind. Bain waited for the other to give him a lead. The initiative had passed, leaving a sense of shame. He had lied to Caroline—to himself even. Now this. He watched Arran cautiously, his hatred of the man bitter.

Arran was enjoying his role. "If you want to smoke . . ." he waited till Bain had his cigarette alight. "You never learn," he said next. "Letting yourself be seen—I recognised you from Pablo's description. Then you'll always ruin a reasonable plan with some theatrical gesture. That shot over my head, for instance. It's just conceivable that without it, you could have marched me off into the woods." He stabbed his stump at Bain. "*If* I had gone. How long have you been in Spain?" He shrugged. "It doesn't matter. Forgetting the drama, you came for money. That's it, isn't it?"

There was still time to put a bullet in the bastard's head. But with three witnesses, he might as well turn the weapon on himself, afterwards. He kept his eyes on the burning ash, his voice low. "For two years, I believed in your loyalty. You knew what a jail sentence would do to me. If I didn't know why you did it, I'd ask you."

Arran pushed his stump out of sight. "Money," he

agreed. He leaned his head back, his face amused. "You'd better spare me all those ethical criticisms. They get one nowhere. What *were* you when I met you?" he challenged. "A sort of colonial Raffles, doomed to spend most of his life in jail. I've *been* to prison once, my friend. Yet I loathe it above everything else. I've never gone back because I *think*." He tapped his forehead with a finger. "If you really want to know, you were expendable, if you remember the word. It was nothing more than that."

Bain fumbled the shells from the automatic, dropping them into his overall pocket, one after another. Then he looked up at Arran, defeated. The man spoke his lines without anger, excuse or bluster. Almost like a scientist for whom the human factor has no value. *You were expendable.* It took more than a few ounces of lead to destroy that kind of inhumanity.

Bain recognised his own weakness. His lively fear of consequences. Fear for his life. This, the other man disdained. Cunning told Bain to let his hatred be seen—to hide only his determination to implement it. "I can't reach you, can I?" he asked slowly. "It means nothing to you that I was a loyal partner—that I'm here in Spain, broke. Because you sold me to the cops?" He probed carefully, remembering that Arran could never know he'd not been taken with the keys. "How do you suppose I got out of the rope you slung round my neck!" He lied with conviction. "There's one thing that escaped your master brain. We were seen leaving Middleburgh House." He jabbed a dirty finger at the other. "Not only *me* but you."

Arran tipped his weight back on the chair, rocking slowly, watching Bain's face. "Indeed?" he said at length. "Do you want me to tell you what happened in that police station! To start with, you were the comic hero you always wanted to be. Why do you suppose it was easy to fill your head with bunk about honour among thieves for two years! You were Staunch To The Last!" He made his voice a parody of Bain's. "I've got nothing to say to you cops!

These keys I never saw before in my life!" he jibed. "And then . . ." he grinned, wagging his head. "Enter the crafty inspector with something culled from page one of the detective's manual. 'A maid saw you from a window,' " he intoned. "At times, Bain, you're such a fool that I'm intrigued to know how you come to be free. Unless you're a jail-breaker." His face suddenly sober, he got to his feet. "You're capable of that, it's true. In which case, I'd have to think about my duty to the authorities."

But the indifference was overdone, this time. The mockery a little too studied. Bain kept his voice steady. "We were seen," he repeated. "The woman's already identified *me*. I don't know whether I'm the half-wit you take me for but the fact remains—I broke out of nowhere. Admittedly, what I've done is as crazy. I'm out of jail on a promise. When Farrell knows I've broken it, chances are that your liberty will last exactly as long as mine."

Arran walked up and down the unlittered part of the hall, using it like a stage. He kept his face averted. Suddenly he stopped. "I've seen Farrell. I've heard him give evidence in a half dozen cases at the Old Bailey. The man's not a fool. He knows when there's a chance to convict." He leaned his back against the refrigerator again and spoke with conviction. "It's just possible that we *were* seen. But unless something connects me with you, I'm in no danger. There is only one unknown quantity." He came across and lifted Bain's chin with his good hand. His voice was gentle. "You're broke and you can never go back to England, is that it?" He clapped Bain's shoulder as if satisfied to answer his own question. "You're a nuisance value, Bain. That's why I intend to get rid of you." He ran his fingers over the filthy dungarees fastidiously, wrinkling his nose at the sweated grime on Bain's face and neck. "Where are your belongings?" he asked.

Bain shut his eyes. Defeat was a welcome darkness where nothing mattered any more. Something beyond reason gave him the wit to answer "Gibraltar."

"Gibraltar?" repeated Arran, slowly. "I'll need—let me see—a day. Come back here, the day after tomorrow." He had the patient benevolence of the kind and old. "I'll have a ticket for Mexico for you. And a hundred pounds. After that if you ever bother me again, my friend, I'll give your problem serious attention." He threw the door open. Outside, the wind still slammed the shutters overhead, changing the freakish pattern of light. "Take your steamroller or whatever it is," he added, "and get to hell out of it! When you come for the ticket, dress like a gentleman and knock." He held out his maimed arm in mock greeting. Bain went past him without answer. Arran's voice was still friendly from behind. "The knocking is important. Remember, I'm a property owner. If you crawl like a thief, I may be tempted to blow your head off your shoulders."

Away from the house, it was better. It had been hard to walk with the uppers of his shoes chafing his cut ankles. He'd left the farmhouse like a horse-whipped tramp. He sat at the side of the track and took off his shoes. He could hear the windows being shut ostentatiously and pictured the contempt on Arran's face. After a while, he walked to the scooter, barefooted, and changed his clothes. Then he rode back to Malaga.

It was after ten and the streets full of people. He parked the scooter in front of the Emperatriz and went up to bed, beyond food. When he had undressed, he used the shower, washing the filth from his body. The light out, he lay on his bed, remembering each humiliation as a man probes a hollow tooth. Experiencing pain as a necessity. Arran grinned from every corner of the room, whispered gently from the pillow under Bain's head. Till Bain rolled on his stomach, hiding his face. After a while, he relaxed and lit a cigarette.

Nothing mattered any more save Arran's destruction. Neither reason nor expediency. And there was still a way to destroy him. Jail him. It wouldn't be easy. There was no evidence against Arran. He wasn't even living in British territory. But back a few years, they'd ridiculed the idea of a single man being able to destroy a fighting ship from the outside. A charge of explosive and a fanatic ready to give his life had changed ridicule to fear. Lulled by the thoughts, Bain sought sleep. At the back of his mind, he remembered that Caroline was in Gibraltar and because of it, the next day a better one.

He dressed with care in the morning, matching a silk shirt to the freshly-pressed mohair suit. Downstairs, he went to the desk. "There's a scooter out front," he told the clerk. "Get somebody to keep an eye on it. I'll be in Gibraltar till tomorrow."

The clerk smiled agreement. "Would you like me to prepare your bill, sir?"

Bain shook his head. For the moment, the bitterness of the night was gone. Beyond the glass doors, the sun drenched the palms in warm light. "No," he said with certainty. "I'll be back tomorrow."

And he would, in spite of the failure of yesterday, he sensed that he had cracked Arran's composure. If only to the point of a promise. In times of stress, Arran's motives were never obscure—only his actions. This offer of a ticket to Mexico was designed to protect one person. Himself. It had been made with a sneer—the mocking disbelief with which he acknowledged danger—but Arran accepted the possibility that he *had* been seen. For him, chance was an enemy to be respected. To be placated for the moment by sending Bain as far away as possible. The important thing was that it was more than an excuse for Bain to return to the Finca San Carlos. It was an order he must obey.

He took a ticket at the bus terminal, changing at the cross-road that led to Gibraltar. At La Linea, the Spanish Customs boarded the bus under the arch that spanned the frontier highway. Without as much as a briefcase, Bain sat indifferent as the police probed string bags and opened cases. There was a white strip of concrete highway between Customs and passport control. It was desolate in the white glare. Weeds climbed the barbed-wire emplacements, to the water's edge. At the end of the causeway, twenty yards separated the frontier posts. On the British side, a red-faced Highlander stamped guard, kilt swinging. A couple of Spaniards stood their guard in the shade, bayonets fixed, their faces under heavy helmets obscured in cigarette smoke.

All passengers in the bus left for passport control. Through the frontier, Bain showed his documents. His police pass was still good for two days. He took a cab from the market place to the Rock Hotel.

She was sitting on the terrace, watching the driveway. As she saw the cab, she ran, calling his name. She moved awkwardly, as always, black hair swinging. He took her in his arms and held her close, frightened by her eagerness.

"Tell me I was good," she said. "*Tell* me!" She held up her mouth.

He bent to kiss her. "You were great," he said quietly. As they went to the desk, he held her arm, glad of its firm pressure. They gave him a room near hers and she fussed as he washed, chiding him for bringing no baggage.

"Where *are* your things?" she asked suddenly.

He pushed her hair aside, his mouth at her neck. "You've asked more questions in a quarter hour," he whispered. She stayed quiet then twisted her head and he saw she was crying.

"I'm glad, Mac. I'm glad." In spite of the tears, she smiled at him.

"I'll tell you what," he said quickly. "We'll make a bargain. Ask me no questions till after dinner tonight and I'll give you no answers."

She went to the mirror and used her lipstick. "All right. Just one question." Her back was turned to him. "Is it good news or bad?"

She was able to make a coward of him with a word. All those jolting hours in the bus, he had told himself that the truth would be easy. But it was a test that he feared and now he avoided her inquiry, ashamed. "Good—bad. Who the hell knows," he said bitterly. "I've almost got enough, Caroline. I'm tired and I'm desperate." His voice cracked and he hurried the words, content to postpone what had to come. "Give me a chance to think and we'll talk later. To-night," he promised. Later he thought. When he'd lie with the worst kind of lie—a half truth.

She shook her hair back, combing its length smooth. "I don't care, darling. Only this time, I'm going to help." She turned slowly, showing her dress. "No comment?" she said.

He sat on the edge of the bed, watching her, his face without expression. "It's new," he guessed. "And blue's your colour."

She came to the bed and pulled his head against her. "It's old," she said. "And you've seen me in it twice." Though she smiled, the nerve worked in her mouth and her eyes were unhappy.

They walked down to the town, their hands brushing without holding. As if each feared the contact. In one of the Indian stores, he bought a razor and toothbrush. In a florist, a sheaf of carnations heady with the scent of cloves. The pavement was crowded. He blocked it, holding the flowers, watching her face as though it were the last time he would see her. "With love," he said gravely and pushed the bouquet in her arms.

They walked up to the hotel without talking. At the door to her room, she turned. "Will eight be all right?"

He nodded. "Eight."

She put the flowers on the floor and held his arms. "If you do love me," she said reasonably, "you'll share this thing with me—whatever it is. That's what love means, Mac."

The word sickened him. He was filled with sudden impatience as if with a game grown boring. "Wait till you know what you're asking to share," he said roughly. "I'll be down at eight."

She took her flowers and closed the door. He stood there, undecided, till a maid came down the corridor. He walked past the woman's curious stare to his own room. For a while, he stayed at the window. Down below, a uniformed attendant was shepherding guests into the hotel car park. The man's arms were pompous in signal but he whipped off his cap to open the car doors.

There it was, Bain told himself. A part of what his father called the Established Order. Shining automobiles, clear county voices, the wet shaven lawns, defying the heat. It was a pattern of life that you followed and to which others aspired. These past few years had never been a tilt at Established Order. Only rebellion at his place in it. Now, none of it mattered. He knew what he had to do. If it hadn't been for Caroline, the acceptance might have given him peace.

At seven-thirty, he tidied himself for dinner, scrubbing the last of yesterday's grime from his nails. Then he went downstairs and sat at the bar. He was irritable. Twice he had words with the barman, the crow-faced colonel who sat on his left. Even the scrape of a chair was annoying him—the tilt of an elbow. He drank two large brandies quickly, watching the door in the mirror.

She wore the white linen dress, her long black hair twisted up over a comb, a pinchbeck necklace round her throat. One of the carnations he had given her was pinned to her shoulder. He slid from his stool to take her hand in his. There was a window table for them in the white and gold restaurant. They ate their meal hurriedly and went out to the terrace. It was empty and he chose two chairs at the far end. He balanced his glass on the cane arm rest and lowered his head in his hands. Upstairs, he'd thought it all out. There could be no more compromise. Not with anything, even Caroline.

When I've finished the drink, I'll tell her, he thought. Like a child, postponing a task, he counted a hundred, watching her. Her skin was dark in the violet light. The gold glinted at her neck. Only her eyes were unfathomable. He emptied his glass deliberately.

"I went to Spain to kill your husband," he said suddenly. "I've lied to you from the very beginning, Caroline. I always meant to kill him. Even . . ." *since I loved you*, he wanted to say. "Even these last few days," he finished.

She moved swift fingers to grab at his wrist. His glass clattered to the ground. "You *fool*!" she said, loudly. A few tables away, a man turned his head from his coffee. She lowered her voice. "What have you done, Mac?" she asked.

He hunched a shoulder. "Nothing. He ran me off his place like a dog. I could have killed him, Caroline. But he wasn't afraid. He just grinned at me. Do you know what that means?"

She hitched her chair closer, holding his wrist as if she thought he might escape her. "You ask me if I know," she said bitterly. "Tell me what happened, the truth," she demanded.

He shut his eyes again, making his confession. Reliving every detail of the scene of the farmhouse till hate choked his voice. When he had done, he waited for the sound of her going. *Christ, let her go!* he told himself. Then he would be rid of his need to scheme and to wound. Brandy glowed in his head and he opened his eyes to stop the spin in them.

She was so close to him that the smell of her hair was strong. "Listen to me," she was shaking his arm gently. "I don't care about the sort of lies you've told me. Oh, Mac—how can you be such an idiot! I can think of nothing except us." Her voice was happy. "Now we can leave this awful place tomorrow. We can go anywhere. Don't you see," she urged. "This was a poison you had to get out of your mind. Now it's forgotten."

He lit a cigarette as an excuse to free himself from her hand. Her touch, even the thought of her was a trap to be avoided. "Nothing is forgotten," he said and he knew that his voice was glad. "If we went away as you say, nothing between us would be worth a damn. This isn't some bloody principle." He tried to explain, wondering at her obtuseness. "You're supposed to know all about love," he reasoned. "Well, you don't hate on principle any more than you love on principle." He shook his head. "As long as I live, I'll remember," he said quietly.

The lights on the terrace came on. Over their heads, the mauve blooms were a clustered canopy. A waiter was moving among the tables. Bain ordered another brandy and drank it in one defiant gulp.

"Come here," she said suddenly. When he made no move, she reached out, putting her palm against his cheek. "You're my love," she said steadily. "Nothing can change that. Nothing. It may be my last chance and I'll fight to keep it. What will you do now?" she asked him.

"Go back to Spain. Tomorrow." He scowled like a man who expects a challenge.

Her fingers never stopped twisting the necklace at her throat. "Then I'm coming with you," she answered.

The last drink had been good. He clapped his hands for the waiter, indifferent to the turned heads. "You're going to stay here," he said with decision. "I'll be back," he said. Unable to control himself, he laughed loudly. As if the words astonished him, he repeated them. "I'll be back, Caroline."

She sat up straight, her face cold with anger. "Stop acting like a spoiled child!" she said suddenly. "How can you *do* this sort of thing to me! It's torture worse than anything Peter ever dreamed of. At least I knew he didn't love me. I just loved him."

"And I *do* love you?" He passed the brandy under his nose, considering the question. Then he tilted the glass. "To my love," he smiled and finished the drink. He concentrated on his words. "I could give you everything you need, Caroline. Promises, assurances. Maybe I'm too tired to lie any more. I dunno. But there it is. I'm going back to settle every debt that I owe. If that's what hate does, maybe it isn't such an empty emotion as people think."

She looked at him, steadily. "And you expect me to wait here—knowing no more than that?"

He hiccoughed then nodded heavily. He was seeing her through a haze and he narrowed his eyes. "The passport," he said cunningly. "Will you give me your word you won't say anything about the passport?"

The deep blue eyes had only pity, now. She nodded her head. "I won't try any more to stop you. I don't think I even want to. You must do whatever you will."

He held her arm tightly through the lounge, willing himself to the elevator. Liquor tricked his mind till the walls of the corridor were those of a jail. At the door to her room, he fumbled for the catch that would close his cell. Then he staggered to the bed and collapsed.

She bolted the door then undressed him. She brushed his clothes, folding them carefully. In the dark, she held his head against her shoulder and lay like that, without tears, till sleep healed the ache in her mind and her body.

SATURDAY

HE WOKE, sore-eyed, and eased himself carefully from the bed. When he found his clothes, he carried them to the bathroom. Stockings hung from the rail of the shower—a girdle on a towel, drying. He dressed quickly and tip-toed across the dark bedroom, his shoes in his hand. She moved in the bed, stretching an arm across the place where he had lain. As he slid back the bolt on the door, the rhythm broke in her breathing. He stood immobile till she was quiet again. Then he opened the door quickly and went out to the corridor. It was empty. Back in his own room, he shaved, ripping the beard from his chin, impatiently.

It was better this way. To leave her sleeping and go. He

had no heart for goodbyes. It didn't matter what label he tied to this feeling he had for her. Pity—tenderness—love. He only knew that it was not strong enough to influence him. She knew it, too. He had no heart to face either her defeat or her courage. Everything he couldn't say, he could write in a letter. By the time she read it, he'd be out of Gibraltar. Just a few desperate days, now, since they'd known one another. Yet she claimed love with a conviction that bothered him. Woman on the rebound, part of his mind told him. Yet he was unable to dismiss her sincerity. One thing was certain. Both he and Caroline needed something more than themselves.

It was eight o'clock. He swabbed his face dry, took his room key and went down to the deserted lounge. Chairs and tables were piled out on the empty terrace. Wet tiles were still drying in the heat of the sun. He took paper and pen and went out there to write the letter. At any moment, she might wake, guess his intentions and come downstairs. Words crowded his mind. It would be easy to combine drama with false nobility. Yet what he was doing was done in revenge. When he had finished, the letter was no more than a recital of his plan, monstrous in its inevitability. He wet the gummed envelope and ran a finger twice along its back. Then he went to the desk.

"My bill," he said to the clerk. He shoved the letter across the counter. "And will you see Mrs Arran gets this when she comes down? It's important that she doesn't have it before."

The man had the fresh courtesy of a new day. "Of course, sir. I'll see to it myself." He pulled a card, made a couple of entries and gave Bain his check.

"There's no chance the letter would be overlooked?" Bain hid his anxiety under the cover of finding the right money.

The clerk's face was faintly pitying as he made change. "Nothing is ever overlooked at the Rock, sir." He pushed the letter into a rack. "I hope you've had a comfortable stay and that we'll have the pleasure of seeing you when you come back to Gibraltar."

Bain looked at the man curiously. There was nothing to see save the professional courtesy of a well-trained hôtelier. "Thank you," he said. "I'll be glad to be back." It was true, he thought. When what goes first is unbearable, the end is accepted with gratitude.

He slipped out of the hotel into the garden and down the steps to the road. If he walked to the town, he'd kill the hour he had to wait for the bus to La Linea. At the bottom of Main Street, the barrack square was crowded with soldiery. He stood with the rest of the passers-by, watching the pipers as they moved round to the head of the formation. First drums rattled the beat, then the high wail of the pipes cut in, keening the wild melody. Behind them the red-faced young Scots strutted, proud-eyed.

Bain turned away, swallowing the memory of twenty Burns Nights, three thousand miles away. The great hall filled with the massed pipe bands. The complete silence as the deep voice read the simple poetry. Lost between his father and mother, himself in the kilt. Smelling the dust from the boards and secretly fingering the hilt of his dirk. Later, the house had been bright with candles while fifty people stamped the reels. And his father, flushed with unaccustomed whisky and emotion, singing in a high, cracked voice.

Though we're far across the sea, yet oor hearts will ever be....
At hame in dear auld Scotland wi' oor ain folk!

He pushed his way through the gathering crowd and boarded the bus. Already, the old women were busy stuffing cigarettes into their stockings, lighters into milk bottles. Using their clothing and bodies as hiding places for contraband. Naïvely, each left some dutiable article in her basket. To be found by the Spanish customs and ignored, shared or confiscated, as the man pleased.

At nine, the bus creaked up the hill to the frontier. Past the airport where he and Caroline had landed, a lifetime ago. London seemed very far away at that moment. At the gates at the end of the white strip of No Man's Land, he left the bus and gave his passport to the control. This was a yokel's face under a cap thick with silver braid. But the eyes had the pebble hardness of a cop at work. The man flipped the pages of the document. His voice was heavy with authority. "You're not a permanent resident of Gibraltar, Mr Ellis?"

Bain showed the police pass. The man glanced at it briefly. "If you're coming back, sir, you'll have to get this renewed. Your week is up today."

The bus had moved, a dozen yards, to the Spanish side of the frontier. Over there, the same sun hit with dazzling intensity. The earth beneath it was the same. It was the men who no longer thought in the same way. Through a gap in concrete and wire, everything changed value. A man's liberty—his life.

As Bain walked to the bus, a dog scurried across the frontier, belly to the dirt. A Spanish soldier shied a rock idly at its ribs, narrowing his eyes as it yelped its way down the road towards Spain. There was no anger in the man's face. Merely the interest of a hunter who follows his shot. Bain took his seat, closing his eyes against the babble and stench. The cuts were sore under his socks and his neck raw with cane scratches. He took off his jacket, throwing it across a basket pungent with garlic.

The long jolting journey back to Malaga was made doubly miserable by his own indecision. One moment, the simplicity of his plan gave him confidence. The next, he remembered Arran's grin, the burning suspicion behind it. Better to phone the Finca San Carlos as soon as he reached Malaga. It would seem natural. Everything had to seem natural. One false move, a word out of place and Arran's cunning would shake the lie from it.

Already, people were struggling with baggage from the racks overhead. They were in the outskirts of Malaga. He walked from the bus terminal to the hotel. Once up in his room, he sat for a while, repeating the lies he must tell till their imagery convinced him. Then he took the phone and called the Finca San Carlos.

Arran's voice answered. He volunteered no more in Spanish than he did in English. There was no identification, neither of himself nor his house—nothing but the forbidding "Yes." As if he would say, "I have the phone in my hand and I'm listening."

"It's me," Bain said quickly. "I just got back from Gibraltar. I've got to see you, right away."

There was silence. Arran passed each word through a filter, and considered the residue. "If it's about the ticket," he said finally, "you'll have it tomorrow. I'll get it sent to your hotel. Where are you staying? I don't know that I *want* to see you, particularly."

"In Malaga—at the Emperatriz," Bain answered. Even at ten miles, the cool clipped voice filled his stomach with a rattling fear. Something stronger yet kept his voice convincing. "Whether you want it or not, I've got to see you. *Right now.*" He lowered his tone, "Caroline's in Gibraltar."

Arran was incredulous. "Caroline! You mean my wife? You're lying, Bain. You're lying!"

Bain could see the thick lip as it curved. "If you think that, you'd better call the Rock Hotel . . . She's registered under her own name." He held the phone away, unwilling to face the test of the next second. Then he heard the voice, tinny with impatience and put the receiver to his ear.

"How do you know, I say? Have you seen her?" Arran was more interested than concerned.

"I've seen her. I've *spoken* to her," Bain said simply.

"Ah!" said Arran slowly. "And what did she have to say, my wife?" He had become patronising.

"I'll tell you that when I see you." Bain loosened his

collar. He would be able to show some of this nervousness later. But there was no margin for error. "It's important for us both."

Arran was suddenly decided. "Then you'd better come out here immediately. Take a cab—do you understand?"

Bain dropped the phone to its rest. If Caroline really believed in the principles she talked about so much, the letter he had left would explain what he wanted of her. He knew that—even at this moment—a call would be going through from the Finca San Carlos to Gibraltar. When she took it, the answer she gave could sink a hook deep in her husband's mouth. It would be Bain who would play it. If she didn't, then she, too, was a liar and the rest without importance. Even the trip to the house in the woods—to meet a man who had no fear—either of being killed or of killing.

He went to the window and looked out. A body smacked from the diving board to the pool. The sound turned the heads of the people in the garden chairs. Leaning down, he tore the keys and the gun from their hiding place. The keys, he locked away in his bag. The second gun, the shells, were stuffed in his pockets. Downstairs, he went out to the garden. Past the mattresses, topped with hot, oiled bodies like so many sausages on a grill, through the iron gate to the beach. He walked fast for a quarter mile. The beach was practically deserted. A dead dog sprawled, teeth bared and body bloated. Around it, the beach beetles blackened the coarse grey sand. Three small girls sat, gravely intent on the spectacle. There was nobody else near.

The beach shelved sharply. Twenty yards out, the water was deep and blue. He started tossing stones at the water, as far as his arm allowed. The small girls watched till they became bored with repetition. They returned to a consideration of the dead dog. Now he started to mix stones with the articles from his pockets, throwing them out till everything was sunk deep beneath the white-caps.

Going back to the hotel, he called a cab. The driver made fast time, grumbling as he turned his vehicle down the gully under Bain's instructions.

As the cab turned into the clearing, Arran rolled over on his elbow, shading his eyes. He was stripped as he had been, two days before. He climbed up, wrapping his stump in a foulard scarf. Then he called and the manservant came to the door to beckon the driver to the rear of the farmhouse. Bain came over and Arran nodded at the beer in an ice-filled tub. "You can give me one, too," he said. As his shoulders moved, the whip scars merged into one another, livid against the copper skin. His eyes never left Bain's face. He held his glass, waiting till the froth had subsided. "You pour beer to the *side* of the glass," he said tolerantly. Then he waited.

Bain threw his jacket on the grass and followed it, holding his head in his hands. He drained his beer and looked up. "She's going to the cops," he said steadily.

Arran took the scarf from his maimed arm, rewrapping it with care. He grinned down at Bain. "Is she? About what? Her husband deserting her?"

Bain stood up. "You don't believe anything, do you?" he asked bitterly. "I know you well enough—you wouldn't have lost a second to phone the Rock Hotel in Gibraltar to check on my story. I'm not pulling a bluff, Arran. Your wife's going to the cops," he said again.

Arran pushed his hand out, to shove Bain away. "Don't bawl at me." His voice was too controlled—too reasonable. "Naturally, I telephoned Gibraltar. You're wrong, Bain. It's only *people* I don't believe in." He shook his head. "I telephoned," he repeated, grinning. He let his glass drop to the ground. He played with it, rolling his foot on the slippery surface. "Do you know what my wife said to me?" he asked suddenly.

Bain bent a little at the knees, crooking his fingers. With the denunciation, he'd go for the throat he decided. The thought was savage but his brain worked coolly. "I know what she said to me," he answered quietly.

Arran nodded. "That she's going to the police. Of course! She made that point with me, as well. Then hung up on me." His eyes were thin streaks of blue. "But what *could* she say to the police? She knows nothing." He jumped swiftly, grabbing Bain's tie with his good hand. His maimed arm, he pushed hard against Bain's throat. He pulled on the tie.

Bain sagged, a hoop of steel round his temples, tightening till the blood drummed in his ears. As he fell to his knees, Arran chopped his neck twice, with the side of his hand.

"What could she say?" Arran snarled.

He sat on the ground. The two Judo chops had paralysed the nerve centre. He moved his head painfully. Then he stood up, blinking. "What did you expect?" he asked hoarsely. "Everything to be as the master-mind left it?" In spite of the agony in his neck, he felt like laughing. Arran was hooked. Deliberately, Bain goaded him. "I went round to your wife the moment I left the police station. She turned out to be a bigger clown than I was, Arran. Pop-eyed with innocence, wondering how you had missed one another at the airport." He rubbed his neck muscles, watching Arran warily. This was no time to be crippled. If needs be, he must defend himself.

"Sit down," Arran said suddenly. *"Sit down!"* he shouted this time, the veins in his temple worms under the brown skin. Once Bain was on the grass, Arran rolled on his stomach. "I know my wife," he said confidently. "She wouldn't be here if someone hadn't brought her."

"*I* brought her. I used her, the way you used me," Bain answered. "I filled her head with crap so I could get money to follow you. Do you know why she bought my ticket to Gibraltar?" Sure of himself, he reached across, tapping Arran's foot. "Because I told her *you* said so. I was supposed to be coming to Gibraltar to meet you and she was to follow. She sat that one out for three days. When nobody sent for her, she came herself. It was as simple as that."

The skin round Arran's eyes crinkled and his mouth was kind. "It's a bit late to say this—I don't even expect you to believe me, Mac, but I'm sorry. For everything. What's done's done. But if I can get you out of this mess, I will."

"You will," Bain said with conviction. "Because now you're in it with me. That much I go for."

Arran's head was down as he pulled a weed from the lawn. He gave the movement exaggerated care—nipping the stalk between thumb and forefinger, flattening the hole he had made, with the heel of his hand. "I'm capable of dealing with my wife," he said quietly, "but I've got to know the facts. I couldn't get them from her—she sounds hysterical. How much do *you* know?"

Bain's voice was steady. "You'd better believe every word of this. She gave me an ultimatum." His eyes were uncompromising as he met Arran's look. "Either I produce you by tomorrow night or she goes to the cops" He shuffled his shoulders. "If she does . . . it'll be what Farrell is praying for. A clue to the second man. My hunch is that if both of us are identified, the cops have a stronger case. Your wife isn't only your problem, Arran. She's made herself mine."

Arran rolled on his back, stretching for another bottle of beer. He tossed it at Bain, waiting for the cap to be knocked off. "You know, I made a mistake about you, Mac," he said suddenly. "The pity is that now it's too late. It *is* too late, I suppose?" he asked slowly.

The pull of the quiet voice was strong—the frankness of pale eyes bright with friendliness. "You're the most dangerous bastard I ever met," Bain answered honestly. "On paper, you've got everything to offer. Guts, brain, appearance. But if you dropped dead this minute, nobody'd bother to say 'too bad!'" He shook his head. "You're going to give me this ticket because I'm an embarrassment to you. OK. Give it to me and let me get the hell out of it.

Save your acting for your wife. I promise you you're going to need it."

Arran sprawled on his back. He shut his eyes and yawned. "You come here to tell me my wife's capable of putting us both in jail. Then you think I'm going to hand you a ticket for Mexico." He rapped his chest with his stump, opening his eyes wide. "Leaving *me* to get us both out of trouble. That's too naïve. You've been at pains to remind me that we're both in this, together. It's something *you'd* better remember," he finished mildly.

Bain turned his body till they were side by side. By the manœuvre, he avoided looking into Arran's face. Even now, Bain mistrusted the man's involved cunning. It was unreal, lying here, next one another. The warm sun on their faces, the breeze from the pines clean and soft. Two men, expediency forcing them to hide a mutual hate. Yet he sensed that Arran's composure was cracked. This shift from violence to cajolery was an admission of fear. Not of death—a man like Arran accepted its finality. But of jail. All his tortuous precautions—even the treachery that had seemed gratuitous were designed to insure Arran against another jail sentence. Now Bain was certain. It was prison that held terror for the other man. With a memory of pain and humiliation that he could never face again. Like a poker player in form, he bluffed.

"Why don't you get your wife to come here?" he suggested.

Arran levered himself up so that he was looking down into Bain's face. The eyes were icy above the grin. "Why not," he agreed softly. "You mean that as long as she lives, she'll be a danger?" Bain made no answer. Arran was persuasive. "Who'd hear a shot if the servants were in Malaga?" He waved his stump at the trees. "Two hundred acres of woods there," he said significantly.

The sun was in his eyes and Bain squinted up. "You'd kill her?" he asked.

Arran roared with laughter. "By God! I had you be-

lieving it! No, I can handle Caroline without killing her.
She has one strong weakness, Bain. She happens to be in
love with me. We'll drive down to Gibraltar tomorrow,
you and I. It'll be the trusted friend bringing me back."
He kept his laugh going too long and too loud. "As you
used to say, there isn't a sour note in the score."

Bain got to his feet. "I'll go to Gibraltar with you—I'll
see your wife with you. But on conditions."

Arran waved a hand. "Don't let all this go to your head.
A ticket and a hundred pounds. That's what you get,
Mac."

He brushed the grass from his clothes. "I want to be
sure I get even that. Before I start for Gibraltar with you,
I want the ticket and the cash. If not, I'm so deep in
trouble I'm liable to tell your wife where you are. And
leave you to handle the jackpot question yourself."

"You'll have them," Arran promised. He was curious.
"You didn't really think I was serious—about Caroline?
Not me, killing?" he persisted.

"I'm sure of it," Bain said. "So sure that I'll never
come back to this farmhouse. You can pick me up at my
hotel."

Arran smiled, shaking his head. "There's something
about that that doesn't ring true. But it doesn't matter.
Be ready at ten. I'll collect you." He shouted for his servant.

It was late afternoon when Bain paid off the cab at the
Emperatriz. Upstairs, he called the garage and arranged
for the scooter to be collected. There was little time, now.
British consulates worked short hours. He was on his way
to the street when the clerk at the desk stopped him.

"Señor Ellis! I had not noticed your return. I have a
telephone message for you." The clerk fished an envelope
from a rack. "From Gibraltar, señor, a lady." He was
taking obvious pride in his English vocabularly. "I had to
say that I did not know when you would be back. The
lady left no name." He gave the envelope to Bain.

He went out to the street and stood in the shade of a palm to open the envelope. The words were in English but written in the elaborate script used by literate Spaniards.

I told you I loved you. If it means waiting five years to prove it, I'll do it.

There was no signature. He tore the note to shreds, dropping them as he walked, as though laying a trail in a paperchase. There was no doubt left in his mind.

He climbed up to the Telephone Building and searched the directory. The British Consulate in Torremolinos was listed under three numbers. He tried the first. A girl answered in English.

"I want to speak to the consul," he told her. "It's a personal matter and urgent."

Her answer was definite. "I'm afraid Mr Burrows never takes calls at this hour, sir. Will you call again tomorrow?"

"I'm a British subject and this is an urgent matter," he persisted.

"I suppose you'd better speak to Mr Murray," she said doubtfully. "If you'll hold on, I'll put you through."

A man's voice cut in, loud and testy. "Consul's office. Murray speaking."

"I want to speak to the consul on a matter of emergency," he said again.

"This is an office, you know," the man answered. "The hours are ten till twelve in the morning, two till four in the afternoon. Saturdays and Sundays, excepted." He managed to give the impression that even those hours were of grace and favour.

It was close in the booth and Bain sagged a little with the heat. The end was too near to be bitched with idiocy. He made an effort to control his temper. "I understand all that," he said quickly. "I've told you this is an emergency. Don't ruin your career by sticking to rules."

"Very well, then." The voice was slightly indignant.

"You had better come here immediately. Ring the top bell in the gate." The phone went dead.

He took a cab out to Torremolinos. The British Consulate perched in the hills behind. It was a white house, built in a half circle round a patio. Moorish windows were almost hidden by creeping vines. On top of the flat roof, a Union Jack flapped from a staff. Heavy iron gates in the tall lime-washed walls opened to a short gravelled driveway. Bain pushed the top bell. After a while, the door at the head of the step was opened. A man stood there, shading his eyes against the sun. When he made out Bain, he sauntered the twenty yards to the gates. In spite of the heat the man wore an Edwardian jacket with double-breasted waistcoat. A high stiff collar gave his scraggy neck the look of a rooster's. He unlocked the gates, re-fastening them once Bain was inside.

"Are you the fellow who telephoned?" he asked. He tore at his vowels, banishing them down his long thin nose. Thick black eyebrows shot up and down with incredulity. Bain nodded. "My name's Murray," the man said. Bain nodded again and followed up the steps to the house.

A door across the tiled hall was labelled WAITING ROOM. Murray opened it. A long counter split the room in two. On the far side, a few desks and files went to the windows. On the near, two wooden forms were backed against the wall. Murray sat on of them, crossing his skinny legs with care.

"Well," he said importantly. "We'd better start by having a look at your passport. I suppose you *are* a British subject?" He narrowed his nose, squinting down its length.

The windows in the room were shut tight—the stuffiness a compound of chalk and bored wasted hours. Bain moved restlessly on the uncomfortable bench. "I'm a British subject, all right," he said suddenly. "But let's not

waste time—there isn't much of it left. You take me in to
see the consul!" He got to his feet.

Murray shot his eyebrows. "Good God, man, don't be
ridiculous! The consul can't be disturbed save in matters
of the *gravest* emergency." He showed unhappy long
teeth as if despairing of Bain's inquiry fitting into that
order. "And I'm the judge of what constitutes an emergency."

Beyond the front door, a typewriter was clicking. A dog
barked in the patio. A heavy-built man showed through
the window, calling to the animal. "Do you read your
English papers?" Bain asked.

The high red forehead creased. "Naturally. Why?"

Bain leaned his back into the edge of the counter, taking his weight on his elbows. "The Duchess of Middleburgh was burgled a week or so ago. I did it." He watched
as the man mouthed the title—like a child learning a
lesson. He waited for shock to show in Murray's face.

Murray ran a finger round the inside of his collar. Then
he stood up. "You can't expect me to disturb the consul
for that!" he said petulantly. "You'll have to go to the
proper authorities."

Bain stood there for an incredulous second. Then he
shoved both hands on the other's chest, knocking him
down to the bench. "You jerk!" he shouted. "Don't you
understand what I'm saying! This is a confession to a
crime in England. And you're telling me to go peddle my
papers somewhere else." He slammed Murray's back
against the white-washed wall. "Take me to the consul!'
He shouted, beating out the words with the other's
shoulders.

As a door creaked behind him, Bain dropped Murray
and turned to confront the newcomer. It was the man
from the patio—short, with a wrestler's shoulders and a
fringe of dirty red hair. "Let's call that enough," he
boomed. "I'm pretty handy at that sort of thing myself."
There was scratching at the door. The man opened it

again. A Doberman bounded in to crouch at it's master's feet, sniffing cautiously at Bain.

Murray was up again, straightening his tie, his face red with indignation. "I'll call the police, Mr Burrows. The man's insane." He edged along the counter till he was behind the consul. "Literally forced his way in here," he complained, "demanding to see you. With some cock-and-bull story about a burglary in England."

Bain half threw a fist in his direction. The consul knocked it up with an arm as hard as his voice. "I said enough." The man smelt of dog and tobacco. He rubbed the top of his scalp, vigorously. "I know what he said, Murray. I should have thought the whole of Torremolinos knows, the way he yelled it." He looked Bain over with interest. Then he motioned towards the hall. "Let's continue this discussion where we'll be a little more comfortable," he invited. He opened the door, putting a large foot under the Doberman's rump, lifting it out of his way. As they went out to the hall, Bain heard him muttering to Murray. "Don't be so bloody hysterical."

The long hall curved left and right, following the line of the patio. Square in its centre, a large framed picture of the Queen hung on the wall. They followed the consul through an open door. It was an English room with battered chairs covered in faded chintz—a desk littered with tobacco cans and tins of cigarettes. A wall safe was open, the keys dangling from the lock. Over the wide empty fireplace were faded pictures of husky young men with bony knees. In the front row of each, a younger version of the consul crouched with a Rugby football.

Burrows pushed a chair at Bain. They sat facing one another, the dog at Burrows's feet. Murray had gone to the window to sit in silence, his popping eyebrows the only sign of life.

The consul pulled a cigarette from a tin and lit it. "Well," he said slowly, "you wanted to see me—I'm listening."

The short smooth hair along the dog's backbone was faintly darker. Bain kept his eyes on it as he talked. "I'm neither a fake nor a lunatic. I've come here to make a statement—a confession, if you like. The Duchess of Middleburgh was robbed, a few days ago, in England. I'm one of the two men responsible."

"Are you, by God!" The consul's voice sounded almost pleased. He scratched the red fuzz over one ear. "A burglar!" He lowered his head, swinging it a little. "You're quite *sure* you're not an escaped lunatic?"

Bain met his look. "What do you think?" he asked.

"I'll tell you when I've heard a little more." Burrows peered through the grey-blue smoke. "This isn't a police station. What made you come to me?"

Suddenly desperate, Bain tore down his socks, showing the cane scabs as if they were answer enough. "I've crawled a mile on my belly, for law and order. This is British territory, isn't it! I'm confessing to a felony committed in England. And you ask me why I come here!" Something in his tone made the dog growl. The consul shushed it to silence. "I'm an informer," Bain said bitterly. "I'm turning myself in, not only myself but a man I'm going to bring into Gibraltar tomorrow. *That's* British, too. Your job's to get the police there from England, in time to grab both of us."

The consul moved in his chair, heavily. "What's your name?"

"Macbeth Bain." There was purpose rather than amusement in the consul's face now. Bain pressed it. "You have the means to contact Scotland Yard in a hurry. Have them get in touch with Inspector Farrell of Gerald Road Police Station. See that he knows that I'm signing a statement in front of you. That I'm going to bring the second man into Gibraltar tomorrow." He pointed a finger. The dog lifted its head, growling again. "The *second* man, don't forget. Farrell will be out on the first plane from London," he promised.

Murray made a sound of exhaustion from the window. The consul bent to scratch the dog's ear. Then he got up, moving easily in spite of his heavy build. "You rather force my hand," he said. "Pour Mr Bain a drink, Murray," he ordered. "Keep him company while we see what we can do for him." He smiled, not unkindly.

As the consul reached the door, Bain called him back. "Mr Burrows! I want you to understand what this is about. You need me—make no mistake about it. Keep the Spanish police out of it."

The consul kept his smile. "Obviously, you're not a student of current affairs, Mr Bain. At the moment, we are not particularly popular with the Spanish police. I can imagine what General Matute might reply if I asked for help in a case like this. You have my word," he finished.

Murray went to the open wall safe. There was gin in it, bottles of tonic, a Thermos filled with ice cubes. Murray mixed drinks with the deftness of experience. He came across to Bain, dropping a twist of lemon peel into the glass. "You don't—ah—*look* like a burglar!" He was throaty with condenscension.

Bain took his drink. The mixture smelled faintly medicinal but he swallowed it with gratitude. "What did you expect?" he asked. "Bill Sykes with a lantern?"

Murray lowered himself elegantly into the consul's chair. He hawked, his face red-veined with the effort. "I meant there isn't much excuse for a chap like you, is there?" He rubbed the tip of one brogue shoe against the back of his sock, furtively.

Bain filled his glass again. "But I haven't made any excuses," he reasoned. His voice was flat. "Look, chum! Don't knock yourself out to make conversation with me. The man said serve the drinks. OK, you've done it. That lets you out." He grinned with malice. He walked over to the open windows. Outside in the patio there were jacaranda trees, hibiscus growing in pots in the flagged courtyard. Beyond the whitewashed boundary of the garden, flat roofs dropped a half mile to the harbour. On the horizon, a ship steamed into the dying sun like a silver toy.

He rested both elbows on the sill. No time at all, now, and he'd be doing just this from a cell window—ears straining for the creak of a patrol's feet outside the door. The barked command. "Geddown from that window!" As if the screw grudged even sight of things he could not dominate. Bain remembered every detail. The granite cell blocks, high on the bleak brown moor. A tortured line, unbroken by trees. Nothing but bog, peat and stone. Mist hid one cell block from another, four months in the year. With the first swirl, the ponies huddled together, tails to the wind. The jackdaws on the chapel, wheeling uncertainly, croaking their anxiety in the darkening sky. This was what he was going back to, but to live through now. Not because of Caroline. A thief's world was peopled with sad-eyed women, promising to wait. But time and expediency proved stronger than desire. The letters became fewer. The heart-pounding calls to the visiting boxes tailed off, till at the end, a decent silence buried all regret. It was Arran's company that would make life in jail worth living. Arran sharing endless indignities, frustrations, till fear cracked his untouchability.

A bell had started to toll in a church tower. Bain turned as the door handle clicked. The dog was first in, then a girl carrying a typewriter. Burrows last of all, the frieze of hair tousled. The girl carried her machine to the littered desk. She folded her hands in her lap and looked everywhere but at Bain.

"Just one minute, Murray." Burrows jerked his head at the hall. The two men went out there for a moment and talked, their voices low. Burrows came back by himself. He poured a long glass from the gin bottle and wedged his behind into a chair. "I didn't think you'd want a bigger audience than necessary," he said. His eyes were curious. He chased the gin round his palate, smacking his tongue. "Ah!" he said thoughtfully. "Macbeth Bain! You've been quite a lad, haven't you?"

The man had as little malice as the dog at his feet. Bain warmed to him. "You've been in touch with Scotland Yard?" he asked Burrows.

The consul nodded. Behind his bluff manner, shrewdness showed. "You were in the navy, they tell me."

"RCN," Bain said steadily.

The consul's head wagged again. "I'm not preaching." He turned to the girl, suddenly. "Wait outside a minute, will you, Miss Russell? Leave your typewriter," he added.

Once the door had shut, Burrows kept his voice quiet, his eyes on the bottom of his empty glass. "Scotland Yard want you all right, Bain. *And* this confession you're going to make. They seem to set great store on it. Presumably, you know what you're doing." He scrubbed one ear with his knuckles. He dropped his tone to a whisper. "If I went out to find Murray, I'd be astonished to find you gone when we came back." He lifted a square chin in the direction of the open windows.

Ban followed the consul's look. Outside, the bell was still tolling, sad with the memory of childhood. Once over that high wall, he'd be safe. There would be no danger from the Spanish authorities. He could even get Caroline out of Gibraltar before the police arrived from England. He heard his own voice, like a stranger's. "I think I'll sit this one out, sir." He moved his shoulders. "If I knew how, I'd say thanks, some other way."

The consul stood up, short necked and solid on his feet. "Right!" he answered briskly. "It's your pigeon! Don't blame me afterwards. You've had your chance. I might tell you that *I* don't know what the hell I'm doing. I wouldn't have made a policeman." He bawled and the girl came back into the room. Burrows flapped a beefy hand at her. "This gentleman is Macbeth Bain, Miss Russell. He's going to make a——" He sought his ear, doubtfully. "Head the bloody thing a *statement*. When he's read it over, he'll sign in our presence and we witness his signature. Right?" The girl nodded. "Four copies," instructed the consul. "Three for us and one for Mr Bain." He eased his feet to the Doberman's back and waited.

Shutting his eyes, Bain talked, dragging back the memory of time, place and method. The typewriter clicked under the girl's quick fingers. Occasionally, her voice was soft in apology and Bain repeated the last few words. When he was done, he sat with his eyes closed till he heard Burrows creak in his chair. He looked up.

Butts cluttered the fireplace at the consul's feet. The dog was at the window, front paws on the sill, snapping the flies. Burrows took a sheaf of clean typescript and dropped it to Bain's lap. "Read it, mister. If it's what you said, sign it."

Bain read the statement back. There was no loophole left. It was all there, from the first day he and Arran had gone to the public library to check on the Middleburgh home. To the moment they'd said goodbye outside the hotel on Sloane Street. No trick for Farrell to be sure of a conviction with a statement like this. There was bound to be pressure from the insurance companies to find out what had happened to the Duchess's jewellery. The cops would run frantic circles in search of the man who had bought it. But there had been no mention of De Rojas. One factor remained to be taken care of. In a criminal case, the testimony of a confederate was not enough to convict a man, unless it was corroborated. Tomorrow, he'd have the best corroborating evidence of all—Arran's fingerprints on the keys that were hidden back at the Emperatriz. It was a matter of time, now, before both he and Arran were lining up in the Reception block in Wandsworth Prison.

He held the pen firmly, steadying the shake in his fingers. When he had signed four copies, initialling each page, the consul and girl witnessed his signature. Bain stuffed his copy of the statement in his pocket. He wanted to rest now for an hour. Then he would go out on the town. This was the last night of liberty for a long time. Let it be something to remember.

Murray was back in the room, long-nosed with irritation. He bent over the girl's shoulder officiously, reading the papers she was sorting. When she had left the room, he perched on the side of a chair. "Queen's Evidence— isn't that what they call it?" he asked unpleasantly. "Fellow saves his own skin and rats on his chums!" His words were the least bit slurred—as if he'd spent the last half hour at the bottle. "It'll be a scandal if the Judge shows a fellow like you leniency."

Bain moved his arms easily. Without too much effort, he could put this guy through the window. The consul was leaning against the mantel, eyes half closed. It doesn't matter, Bain thought. Nothing matters except getting Arran's body across the frontier tomorrow. "I go one better than that, Murray," he said quietly. "I don't mind giving my own hide to get someone else's. Remember that before I twist your head off. Mr Burrows!" The consul's eyes were suddenly wide and very blue. "What time are the police going to be in Gibraltar?" Bain asked.

"Seven o'clock in the morning," Burrows answered. "I gather your friend Inspector Farrell will be among them."

"Goodbye, then, sir." Bain put a hand out.

"There's just one paper I'd like you to sign before you go. It's a personal matter," Burrows said. "For my own records."

"For you, sure," Bain replied.

The three men walked to the hall. As they climbed the shallow stairs, the consul grunted. "Weight costs wind," he complained. "Down there!" He motioned along the corridor. Rush matting covered the square green tiles. "My own room's up here," he wheezed. "A man gets lazy without a woman. I seem to spend all my time in one room." He unlocked a door on his right. "After you," he invited.

As the door handle turned, Bain moved towards it.

With sudden force, the whole weight of the consul's shoulder took Bain in the back. He sprawled forward, hitting the floor of the dark room with his palms and his knees. As he started to his feet, the key turned in the lock outside. He bellied across the room and put his ear against the faint slit of light at the bottom of the door. He could hear the consul's heavy breathing. A foot slammed against the wood, shocking Bain's ear drums. Then Burrows roared as if he were on the bridge of his ship.

"Are you listening, Bain! I don't want any trouble from you, do you understand?"

He hauled himself up, turning the handle as he moved. The door did not budge. The air in the room was stale, as though the window had been closed for weeks. His eyes adjusted, picking out the shape of a bed, a tallboy. "I'm listening," he answered.

"You're going to stay here till the Scotland Yard officers come for you tomorrow," Burrows called. "Any jiggery pokery and you'll spend the night in the cellar. Do you understand that?"

He leaned his head against the door jamb, sick with defeat. He made one last effort as the feet shuffled outside. "You don't know what you're doing! This other man won't move an inch without me! This is the craziest thing!" There was no answer. He shouted in desperation, pounding on the door with both hands. "It's *illegal!*" he yelled, "*Illegal!*" He swung a fist at the door, unconscious of bleeding knuckles.

Burrows's voice was edged with exasperation. "Get one thing out of your head, Bain. Nothing illegal's going to happen to you while I'm here. You know the position as well as I do—if you don't, you're a bigger bloody fool than I take you to be. Scotland Yard want you handed over to the Spanish authorities. Do you know what that can mean? Weeks kicking about in some filthy Spanish prison while they all talk about extradition. I told you I'd avoid that and I'm keeping my word. Inspector Farrell will be here tomorrow. You'll either go back to Gibraltar with him—or *he'll* call the local police."

He licked his dry lips. There was no answer to make. Tomorrow, it didn't matter whether he went with Farrell or the Guardia Civil. Either way, it would be too late. Arran's nose for danger was long. He wouldn't put a foot on British territory, alone. And if Farrell were to apply for an extradition warrant on the strength of the statement, there'd *be* no contributory evidence—no finger prints on the keys. With his kind of money, Arran might live out his life, blocking one legal play after another.

Burrows was shouting, "Are you all right in there?" Bain heard him add to Murray, "See if the lights are on, man!"

The high choked voice answered, "No, sir." Then Murray called through the door, "Put the lights on and settle down. Settle down, now!"

Bain slammed his fist at the door again with the hope that Murray's ear was against it. Then the steps scuffed along the matting and the corridor was silent. He groped till he found the light button. He was in a stark room with limewashed walls. Dark oiled beams cut the ceiling. Blankets were stacked neatly at the foot of the two beds. There were no sheets. A pot of faded flowers stood in a niche. One bare wall was decorated with a panoramic photograph of the fleet off Spithead. He opened the drawers in the tallboy, the clothes closet. They were empty. The window embrasures were deep on this floor. First glass, then iron, then shutters. The heavy grille made the guest room as secure as a cell.

He kicked off his shoes and moved on the stone floor without noise. The door was cut in lateral planks, inches thick and jointed on the outside. He could see through the empty keyhole to the corridor. Burrows had taken no chances. Short of battering down three hundredweight of olive wood, there was no way out of the room by the door. Yet somehow it had to be done. Either through the door or the window. Once past the consulate walls, he would be in no danger. A man like Burrows kept his word. If he didn't—well, the police would be looking for Macbeth Bain, not Ellis.

He emptied his pockets on the bed. It was a sorry pile. Not as much as a nail file that he might use. He cut the lights and opened the glass panes. Pushing his arm through the grille, he unhooked the shutters and threw them wide. Immediately underneath, a tiled canopy hung over the front door. The patio spread left and right in front of it. Jacarandas hid the gravelled driveway and iron gates to the road.

Over treetops and flat roofs, the sun still glinted on the distant water. But up here, the fold of the hill was in shadow. Already, the two torch lights flanking the door were burning. With nightfall, the front of the house would be as bright as day. He checked his watch. It was almost seven. He stretched himself out on the bed nearer the window and drew his knees up to his chest. There was a persistent gripe in his stomach. Fear, he told himself. He had to dominate it, somehow. It was too easy to accept defeat—flop there like a sheep awaiting the knife at its neck. This was only a room in a house. A couple of men and a dog couldn't turn the place into a jail. He'd had his chance, a few minutes ago. Downstairs, in front of those open windows. He could have been on his way south, by now, to join Caroline. And then what, he reasoned. Carry Arran on his back for the rest of his life! No. He'd got precisely what he'd asked for—only twenty-four hours too soon. There was nothing more he might expect from Burrows. Now, the guy would do his duty with the relentlessness of his kind.

After a while, the pain went from his stomach. He lay still on the bed, listening. Straining, as he'd done in a cell, for the unfamiliar sound that could mean a threat to his well-being. Then feet sounded in the corridor. As the key hit the lock, Bain rolled over to face the opening door.

Murray came in, carrying a tray of food, awkwardly. He posed it on top of the tallboy. The consul followed, carefully locking the door on the inside and pocketing the key.

"There's some grub there and a bottle of wine." Burrows stopped at the foot of the bed, swinging his head like a bull. Openly, he checked the walls and the window. "You'd better make the most of it, Bain." His mouth perched on the beginning of a smile and his voice was not unfriendly.

Bain stared up at the consul as if he might will the man to reason. But he made no answer.

"He probably prefers skilly, sir." Pleased with himself, Murray carried a fork to the window. He tapped the bars, knowledgeably, cocking his head as the metal rang true.

The consul ignored Murray. He lowered his weight to the bed and the springs groaned. "It's a little foolish, going on like this, Bain," he said. He rattled some coins against the key in his trouser pocket. "You've tied my hands, you know."

Bain scowled. "Why do you think I made that statement, because I've got religion—or because I *want* to go to jail?" He pulled himself up and leaned back against the bedhead. "If this other guy goes free, everything I've done merits one large horse-laugh. Do you have any idea what that's doing to me?"

Burrows pursed his mouth, giving the question fair consideration. "You came here," he said at last. "I didn't ask you to come. Now I'm bound by Home Office instructions. My orders are to turn you over to the Spanish authorities for extradition by the Scotland Yard people." He moved his heavy shoulders doubtfully. "Possibly I'm sticking my neck out but this way seems better for everybody concerned." The consul slapped Bain's foot. "I wouldn't worry too much about this other fellow. These policemen are persistent chaps—they'll nab him, sooner or later."

Bain looked up at the red beefy face and knew it was hopeless. To this decent oaf, a man like Arran would be incomprehensible. Burrows lived in a world of fair-play, an occasional excursion into sentimentality, his only conscious failing.

"All right," Bain said. "Forget it!"

"And you'll give this Farrell man no trouble tomorrow?"

"I'll give him no trouble," Bain said.

"Right." The consul was up. He grunted as he leaned his weight on the window grille. "There's just one last thing," he said casually. "I try to do one thing at a time and do it thoroughly. I'm going to keep you here tonight if it means sitting on your head. I don't expect you to give me your word that you'll try no nonsense." He pushed a large hand through the bars, pointing. "That dog of mine's trained to keep Spaniards out of the garden. At night, he's free in the grounds. And he's savage. That's in case you've got some means of getting through these things with your teeth!" He walked over to the door and unlocked it. When the consul was done, he said "Good night, Bain!"

It was impossible to withhold respect from the man and Bain slid from the bed. "Good night, sir," he said steadily. "If I've drawn more than I expected, I don't hold you responsible for it."

The door was refastened. He sat on the side of the bed, eating the cold meat and salad. The wine was red and strong. He drank half the bottle. When he was done, the dozen or so breaks in his skin were unnoticed. The gripe in his belly forgotten. He put the light out and peered through the keyhole into the corridor. It was in darkness. Then he went back to the bed, loosened his tie and willed each part of his body to relax. He dozed like that for a while till the alarm in his brain awakened him.

The sky was pinpointed with stars. The front door lights threw the pattern of the grille, elongated, on the ceiling. The only sound was the rasp of the grasshoppers in the undergrowth, outside. He went to the window and pushed his hand through the trellised metal. Quietly, he pulled the shutters close. Then he switched on the light in the room, draping the fixture with his handkerchief. Had it been cast, a heavy blow would have fractured the grille. But this was tough, wrought iron, embedded deep in the stone embrasure.

They had left him a knife and fork to eat with. He scratched at the cement round the bars with the prongs of the fork. He might as well have used his nails. The door was even more hopeless. Not a hinge was visible. All were set on the inside of the jamb. The box of the lock had been inserted in the thickness of the door. He could see no screws he might work on. He hung his jacket on the door handle, blocking the keyhole view from the corridor. Then he went back to the bed and slumped there, probing the room for a weak point.

Spanish houses were built for the occupants to stay cool. Walls three feet thick insulated the interior from the blaze of the day. Ceilings and doors were in proportion. Burrowing through them was a job for a man with a life sentence. Had the door been vulnerable, breaking through it would have put him in the corridor. He still had no idea where either Burrows or Murray slept. Presumably there were servants. And always the dog.

The window was his only chance. Beating it was going to make noise. With any luck, the noise that awakened the household would mean that he was through the window. The door opened inward. He had to wedge it. He swung his hand idly, fingers probing the canvas that covered the mattress support. It was wood. As the thought struck him, he sprung from the bed in haste and pulled off the box spring mattress. Then he ripped the canvas from the framework of the support. The sides were made of inch thick planks, nine inches wide, six feet in length. Their ends were mitred and secured with screws, their heads still bright and unrusted. Wooden wedges reinforced the inside angles.

He tore a blanket in strips and wrapped one round the knife handle. He went to work on the screws. Twice, the flexible blade bent, then snapped at the end. At four inches long, it made a rough but effective screwdriver. He leaned weight on the tool. Four screws creaked out of the wood. The bed side was free. He broke the glue on the corner wedges and jammed them into the crack of the door. One above, the other below the lock. Sweating, fearful, he stayed a while at the door, listening. He could hear no more than his own harsh breathing. Very gingerly, he tipped a chair-back under the door handle. It jammed on its hind legs. With that and the wedges, anyone trying to burst through in a hurry would be held for valuable seconds.

He carried the plank to the window. It was useless, too wide at the end to pass through the iron arabesques. His tongue was dry and bitter and he tipped the bottle, rinsing his mouth with the rough, red wine. Where the tiled window sill met the inside wall, it formed a sharp edge. He held the knife loosely, between finger and thumb, tapping the length of the blade on the tile, notching the steel. Then he started a diagonal cut across the plank end, using the knife as a makeshift saw. It was slow, hard work. Broken by trips to the door, to the window. Listening for some-body else's strained breathing, cutting fresh teeth in the soft, mild steel. It was an hour before he was through the wood. His ripped knuckles bled where he had scuffed them again on the plank.

But the wood had a point now. An end that he was able to push six inches through the grille. Despite the need for haste, he took his time choosing a point for leverage. With the noise he must make, he would have time for two or three wrenches, at the most. He took his jacket from the door, hanging a blanket in its place. His shoes he stuffed in his coat pockets. When he went through this window, everything that must go with him had to be at hand. He piled the rest of the blankets against the ironwork, to deaden the sound.

He lifted the plank, guiding it through the iron with his tongue, as a child does a pen on paper. The wood bit into a niche near the edge of the framework and poised there, wedged firmly. He took a deep breath and wrenched, twice, towards him, till his arms cracked with the strain. Then away, toes digging into the floor, his chest against the timber. In the quiet night, the noise was sudden and loud. He hung there for a second, getting his wind. The iron had bent, biting into the wood. Cement flaked where the grille was sunk in the stone.

He wrenched again, desperately. There was a clatter as he heaved back. The grille sagged, the two irons on the left, its only supports. Jerking out the plank, he battered the iron with its butt. Beyond the door, he could hear the sound of people running. Burrows's voice, loud in inquiry. He grabbed his coat and clambered up on the sill, unhooking the shutter. Leaning his shoulder against the grille, he shoved. It bent out, leaving a gap big enough for him to go through.

He crouched there on his heels, framed in the window. The flagged patio was bright beneath. If he jumped a little to the left, he would land in a flower bed. The chair under the handle clattered to the floor. Someone was hurling his weight against the door. It could only hold for seconds with the wedges. As he heard Burrows yell his name, Bain lifted on his haunches for the fifteen feet jump. Something moved in the shadow beyond the jacaranda. It was the Doberman. The dog loped into the light, its head long on its neck. It stopped outside the front door, staring up at the window. As Bain moved, the dog snarled, backing a little to get a better view.

The portico over the door was no more than six feet below. He dangled his legs in space, turned over on his stomach and lowered himself to the portico. He looked down. He was standing on a narrow tiled shelf, five feet long. The dog was jumping up at him, front paws thudding against the door. Bain went down on his knees. Leaning out, he smashed both lights with a shoe. There was another window above, to the left of his own room. The shutters were open and the room in darkness. He reached up on his toes till his fingers touched the iron. Digging his feet into the cracks in the stone, he hauled himself up to the sill. In the darkness beneath, the dog still jumped in Bain's direction growling.

If he used the ironwork as a step, the flat roof above would be within reach. Steadying himself against the wall, he made a sudden snatch at the coping. As they scored the stone, his nails split. Then slowly, with weakened muscles, he pulled himself up to the coping. He hit it and rolled over to drop on the roof, exhausted. He could hear Burrows leaning from the window underneath, shouting.

"This way, Murray! He's gone for the gate!" The front door burst open. Footsteps pounded across the patio. The dog followed, whining. He pressed his cheek into the rough cement. Though he had smashed the bulbs over the door, a sliver of moon gave light to the garden. If he pulled himself higher than the three-inch coping, his body would be silhouetted against the white wall.

He lifted his head, a fraction. They were using flashlights on the top branches of the jacaranda trees. Burrows's voice was loud, directing the search. A yellow disc hit the end of the roof. It moved slowly along the coping. As it passed overhead, he held his breath. Burrows called to the servants in Spanish. They crashed through the undergrowth, fanning out to the wall.

Squarely over the front door, the flagstaff showed, black against the silvered sky. A wooden hatch was at its base. He crawled a dozen yards on his stomach. If there were a bolt or padlock on the other side, he was finished. Pushing the heel of his hand under the cover, he shoved. It moved. Only its weight held it down. In front of the house, the servants still thrashed about in the flower beds, shouting encouragement to one another, thudding their sticks against the tree trunks. Once, Murray yelled with pain, cursing the servants to silence.

Bain crawled to the blind side of the hatch. He turned on his back and used both hands to heave up the cover.

Then he propped it with the broken knife and peered cautiously into the hole. The corridor was a dozen feet below. He could see the matting in the dim light from the open door of his own room. He took the weight of the hatch on his shoulder and swung his legs over the hole. For a second, he hung by one hand, using head and free arm to prop the cover again. Then he dropped to the floor. He inched along to the head of the staircase. In front of the open door, lights burned in the hall. Shouts and the noise of running men came from all round the house, now. Past the white glare of the hall, the shadows of the passage were a refuge. With luck, all the servants would be in the grounds. It was a chance he must take.

A heavy vase was on a ledge on the stairs. He dumped water and flowers to the floor, holding the base of the vase like a truncheon. He paused on the last tread. The garden was clear, beyond the door. He ran across, slithering on the tiles, and crouched in the darkness of the passageway. At his elbow, the painted sign on the door was just discernible. It was the room where Murray had first taken him. There was no key in the lock. He pulled the door shut behind him and rammed one of the forms between it and the counter. Flashlights were sweeping the front of the house again, covering the first-floor windows, then the second. Murray's voice sounded suddenly, shrill with excitement.

"He's inside, sir! He's gone back in the house!"

Bain crept behind the counter, moving as if the tiniest noise must betray him. Fascinated, he watched the window, fingers gripping the vase. He crouched there, cracked-lipped. The light would come through the glass in a second. The form buttressed the door—a mute informer to his presence in the room.

Burrows pounded across the patio. The two men were no more than a few feet beyond the windows of the waiting-room, facing the front door. Though the glass was shut, Bain could hear the dog growling. Burrows throttled his voice to a rattling whisper. "Where—*where?*"

"See where he went up over the portico!" Murray said with triumph. The reflection of the light skipped the waiting-room windows, travelling upwards. "I'll shine the torch on the grille in front of my room. There's a piece of cloth on the bar, there. Do you see, sir?"

Bain's fingers felt the stuff of his jacket, mechanically. He probed till he felt through to the lining. A strip was ripped from an elbow. Now it must hang in the full beam of Murray's flash.

"There he is! On the roof!" Burrows shouted. Both men charged through the front door. Barking, the dog followed them, claws scraping the ground for traction.

Bain went over the counter. Flat against the wall, he looked out to the garden. His hand was already on the window catch. Half a dozen servants stood on the patio, undecided, the two women clutching one another's hands. Then a stocky man shouted *"Vamanos!"* Rapping his stick on the flags, he led the rest into the house.

The window opened creakily, letting sweet air into the stuffy room. He swung himself out, careless of the crushed hibiscus. Hugging the wall, he ran to the north end of the house. Past the jacarandas to the boundary wall. He sprang for its top, kicking for impetus. He chinned himself, rolled and for a second lay full length, facing the house. Lights moved across the roof. Bodies showed briefly as men ran shouting from one end to the other. He lowered his legs and dropped to the dirt road beyond.

He went down the hill, aching muscles pushing his feet into a slow, desperate trot. He covered forty yards before he realised he was wearing no shoes. Holes gaped in the soles of his socks. The road dropped steeply in front of him. There were no street lights up here. Villas hidden behind forbidding walls showed no sign of life. A road branched off to the left. Farther down, another, to the right. The whole hillside was a dormitory of solid Spanish citizens.

He sat at the side of the road, pulling his shoes on. Water

was running behind him, in a stone channel. Oleanders covered the wall, like peacocks with outstretched wings. As he heard the sound of a motor, he forced himself into the foliage. The car came down the hill, slowly, and he lay still. Spider webs covered his neck and the croak of the bullfrogs was deafeningly near. The car passed, fifteen feet away, headlights brilliant. The dusty road was clear—a cat scurrying for shelter. The plaque showed over the tail-light of the car. White lettering bold on a black background. CORPS CONSULAIRE. He heard Burrows say something and the driver cut both lights and motor. The car rolled down the gradient, its only noise, tyres in the dirt and the creak of its chassis.

He stayed where he was, washing away the dirt and the blood from his hands and face. Then he stood on the crown of the road, staring down after the car. A quarter mile below, it moved through the network of lanes, its lights bright again. He jogged down to the town, keeping to the narrowest paths, the darkest byways. Hiding whenever he heard a voice or the sound of a motor. A late bus took him to Malaga. It was one o'clock when he turned the corner by the bull ring. The pavement cafés were still crowded. Flamenco music blared from a dozen loudspeakers. Head down, he crossed the avenue and cut down to the deserted beach.

The back of the Emperatriz Hotel was in darkness save for the restaurant. He dragged his feet along the rough track to the gates. Up to now, it had been a clear-cut struggle—if you could forget the question of legality. The consulate had been a jail. Burrows and Murray, jailers he'd robbed of power by breaking out. Official caution would prevent them from touring the hotels in search of him. But he had a sudden picture of Burrows on the end of a phone —sleepy-eyed night clerks searching their registers. He had less fear of the Spanish police. But he'd be safer if he could reach his room without passing the desk.

The iron gates were both shut and locked. It took an

effort to crawl over them. Using the palm trees as cover, he reached the swimming-pool. The water glinted, dark and oily in the moonlight. There were wraps, swimming costumes and towels, drying in the cabins. He stripped, donning a damp slip. His head was hanging with fatigue. He stood there a moment, shaking it. Then he lowered himself into the water. Turning on his back, he floated, the stars over his head. He had no weight. The cool water cradled him, slapping gently over his nostrils and mouth. Suicide would be a relief if you could go out like this. He shut his eyes, arms outstretched, the breeze nudging his body to the side of the pool. As his hands touched the glazed surface, he rolled over and splashed the length of the water. Then he dried himself, wrapping the contents of his pockets in the wet towel. He threw his clothing in a garbage can behind the cabin and walked up the restaurant steps in a borrowed robe.

The French doors to the garden were locked. He could see stacked tables beyond the glass. A group of shirt-sleeved waiters sat round a pot of coffee. Their heads were bent, following the dice on the table in front of them. Bain rapped loudly on the window pane. Again and again till, at last, one of the men turned his head. Bain put his hand flat against the glass. The man came over to the door. For a moment, he stood there staring, then unlocked it. Courtesy blocked the question that showed in his eyes.

Stumbling in Spanish, Bain sought to give the situation reason. "I swim long and late," he said. "And the doors were closed."

The man stood to one side, to let Bain pass. His face was satisfied. As Bain walked by the table, there was a chorus of *"Buenos noche, señor!"* and the waiters went back to their game.

He climbed the half flight to the lobby. The night clerk was at the desk. Head turned, elbows on the counter in front of him, he was reading a newspaper. Moving without sound on his bare feet, Bain crossed the lobby to the staircase. He took the elevator from the second floor. He still had no room key. But the past few years had left a legacy of almost unconscious observation. Impressions that were stored as a chipmunk hoards nuts. The gleam of a diamond—the turn of a head in a crowd—the shape of a key. Four or five times, he had passed the chambermaid about her daily duties. He walked the length of the corridor, recapturing the impression. Outside a door without number, there was a white cupboard. He pulled the handle —the doors were locked. He put a knee against the wall and heaved. The doors swung open. The tongue of the lock still out but rendered useless by a forgotten bolt. Aprons hung on the hooks. At the end, a bunch of pass keys. He took them and opened his door then replaced them in the cupboard. He shut the door by fitting lock to cup and pushing both panels inwards.

He bolted his door and left the light off. He scrubbed his teeth mechanically and laid out his clothes for the morning. Surely now he was safe. Any inquiry for Bain would be answered negatively. If the description fitted a client called Ellis, Burrows must still draw a blank. His room key still hung over the night clerk's head. It was too late for the consul to stop Farrell's trip to Gibraltar. The plane had been in the air for a half hour. But by now, his escape would be known to the authorities on the Rock. Before they could decide what to do, he'd have Arran over the frontier. He slept with the keys in his hand, moaning a little as the moonlight crept to his pillow.

SUNDAY

THE ROOM was bright with morning sunshine. He stood at the window for a while, remembering his escape from the consulate. He took little interest in the memory. There'd be few who would appreciate the irony of the situation. It wasn't as though the Duchess of Middleburgh was some stockbroker's wife. For all he knew, she was able to make her complaint at Cabinet level. Needled by pressure from above, the Assistant-Commissioner must have given the job priority. All over town, cops would be yanking suspects from their beds, tapping telephones, searching houses. Farrell's personal hunch that Bain was responsible meant nothing without proof. That's how things had stood when he'd walked into the consulate—ready to surrender not only himself but Arran. Yet if society had had its way, his confession would have done nothing but provide Arran with extra protection.

He rang room service for breakfast. He no longer feared the consulate. By now, Burrows would have closed his report on an incident he found distasteful. He ran a consulate, not a jail. That last cruise down the dark hill had been taken as the man might have taken a twelve bore to the moors. The thrill of the chase was strong and, to a man like Burrows, satisfying even if there were no kill.

Farrell was another proposition. He'd take the confession—Bain's escape from the consulate—and give them their proper values. He was a cop who knew his thieves. Then, baggy-trousered and sucking his stinking pipe, he'd go quietly about his business. At this moment, Farrell was probably organising a reception committee for the pair of them in Gibraltar. A phone call would make his job still easier.

When he had packed, Bain made a bed of cotton in an empty cigarette tin. If he used this to hold the keys from Middleburgh House, Arran's fingerprints would stay fresh and sharp. These days, just a segment of one print was enough for the Yard's Forensic Laboratory. He dropped the tin into his jacket pocket, keeping the keys loose. It was after nine. He sat on the bed and waited. This was like being on bail—killing time just before you surrendered yourself in court. Sensory impressions were strong, those last few moments. Almost, as if, subconsciously, you were storing them against the flat drab future. Then you walked down to the cells beneath the dock, your head a buzz-saw of testimony and rebuttal.

There could be no chance of an acquittal for Arran. His own confession showed exact knowledge of the other man's movements. An account for which Arran had no alibi. Now everything pointed to the man's guilt. The confession, his flight from the country. And the keys. There would be expert testimony that the keys had been used in the robbery and it would have Arran's prints shown on them.

He pictured the scene at the frontier. Once he had made this phone call to Gibraltar, Farrell would take no chances. A police car would be tucked out of sight, somewhere behind the Customs building on the British side. The detective-inspector's voice sounded in Bain's mind, ominous with formality. "You are Peter Arran? I am going to arrest you under the terms of the Fugitive Offenders Act."

It wouldn't be then that Arran would crack. He'd simply put the pinch down to Caroline—treat it as a hysterical denunciation that could still be explained at the proper time. But later—in the cells at Irish Town Police Station, he'd know about the confession. Farrell might even show him the keys.

Unconsciously, Bain nodded approval. There was no longer any question of avoiding the consequences of his acts. Nor had he any desire to do so. He saw no further than the start of misery that his partner must share. He remembered Caroline uneasily. With shame and pity mixed. At least the lies were done with. His own future was in the hands of the judge, a thousand miles away. She had no real need of him for happiness. Free of Arran, her life couldn't miss being better. Her happiness was what he wanted, he convinced himself. Even though he was not prepared to meet its price himself.

It was getting on for ten. He carried his bag down and paid the bill. When he had left the suitcase under a tree in the front of the hotel, he walked up the avenue a few yards to a bar. Then he called Police Headquarters in Gibraltar. Minutes passed as the operator made the connections. He kept his foot in the door, propping it open, so that he could watch the road towards Rincon de la Victoria. Arran was never late.

"Irish Town Police Station." It was a disinterested voice—as if the owner was too long bored with reports of stray dogs, chimneys on fire, rowdy neighbours.

"I want to speak to Detective-Inspector Farrell, if he's there," Bain said.

"Detective-Inspector Farrell, sir? There's nobody here, that name," the man answered.

Streetcars and buses block his view of the hotel entrance. Any moment, Arran might arrive. Bain wasted no time with explanation. "Get a pencil and paper," he said quickly. "My name's Macbeth Bain. You've got that? Somewhere in Gibraltar, there's a London detective. Inspector Farrell. He'll have come in on this morning's plane. Get this message to him and you won't have to worry about promotion. Say that I'll be at the frontier at La Linea between twelve and one. With Arran. Remember that— it's important. *With Arran*," he repeated.

He waited till the cop had read back the message. Then, throwing change on the bar, he dashed through the traffic to the hotel garden. Under the date-palm, he turned his chair east. Hidden from the hotel entrance, he watched the traffic beyond the low wall. It was a couple of minutes after ten when the Jaguar rounded the bend. It stopped across the street. Arran stayed in the car, watching the hotel.

Bain tossed his bag over the wall and vaulted after it. He made his way over to the car, approaching it from the back. In the driving mirror, Arran's face showed nothing but irritation.

"Get in, for God's sake," he said irritably. "This sliding round corners has gone to your head." He was wearing a pale grey suit and dull red tie. As Bain took his seat, Arran studied the line of his jaw in the mirror, touching the skin tenderly. Then, satisfied, he twisted so that he faced Bain. "You'll have to drop this habit of creeping up on people. It will get you into trouble. Even in Mexico. *Especially* in Mexico," he emphasised. He started a grin, his top lip thickening. "Christ!" he said with feeling. "You look a mess. You know, I don't think you get enough sleep these days, Bain." He touched a button and the motor whirred.

"I get all I need. Did you bring the ticket and the cash?" Bain made his voice hard, letting the scowl stay. He knew the mannerism irritated the other but it seemed natural under the circumstances.

Arran's right sleeve flapped as he pushed it towards the glove compartment. "Still the disbeliever," he jibed.

It was all there. The useless ticket to Mexico City. A thin sheaf of five-pound notes. Bain pushed them into an inside pocket. "Let's get going," he said. "Your wife will be getting anxious."

Arran held the wheel with his good hand and found the right gear with his stump. The Jaguar slid into the stream of traffic.

They drove in complete silence. Bain remembered other drives they'd taken together. Winter days, with the fields stiff with hoar-frost, as they drove down to someone's house in the country. The crunch of leaves underfoot as they moved a ladder from outhouse to darkened bedroom window. The way they had crouched outside a dining-room, peeping through slitted curtains at a fire-lit interior where strangers sat, warm and secure. Then the slow climb up to the bedroom. Under his weight, the ladder shifted in the dirt of the flower bed. But at the bottom was Arran. Arran the reliable, the confident. His hand silently signalling danger or triumph. Each move, then, had been made with a certainty born of mutual trust.

Bain sneaked a look at his partner. Already they were past the western approaches to Malaga. Reaching the straight bit of highway at the military airfield, Arran drove at speed. His mouth was a little thinner under strain as he forced the low-slung car round the badly graded bends. There was still an air of absolute assurance in Arran that Bain found disquieting. He felt as though he was sitting next to a man driving to his own funeral—but a man who would be inwardly certain of beating the coffin.

When they reached the top of the long slope down to Marbella, Arran stopped the car. Pines grew thick to the highway's edge. Over to the right was a log cabin bar and gas pump. "A beer, I think," said Arran pleasantly. The skin on his face was burned brown, his copper forehead damp in the fierce sunlight. By contrast, his eyes were bluer, paler and colder. He looked at his watch. "We can do it in an hour from here."

Bain watched the elegant grey shoulders as his partner walked over to the bar. Letting Arran out of sight—if only for a second triggered a tumult of doubt in his mind. An hour ago, his plans had seemed inevitable. Now, under the spell of the other man's personality, they were childish and ineffectual. Maybe this very minute, Arran was standing in the bar, smug with secret knowledge. Waiting for Bain to betray himself. As Bain stared at the bar door, he switched the keys to his right-hand pocket. After a minute, Arran came out. He had a bottle of beer in his hand, the other tucked under his right arm. He sat in the car and waited for Bain to pour the two glasses.

"I've been thinking," Arran said suddenly. "It may be an idea to phone Caroline from the Spanish side. She could come over to La Linea by taxi." He drained his drink, savouring the tang of the ice-cold beer. "Otherwise it means going through four sets of customs with the car. Just for an hour or so."

Bain fished for imaginary cork in his glass, rather than face the other. He heard his own voice, astonished at its control. "That's for you to decide," he was saying. "I don't give a damn, one way or the other. I've got my ticket. I can get to Tangier for the connection as easily from

Algeciras as from Gibraltar." He capped the empty beer bottle carefully with his glass. "You know your wife better than I do. If you're sure you're going to be able to get a woman in her frame of mind over to La Linea. *And* deal with her in an hour or so . . ." He hunched his shoulders.

Arran touched the horn. A man came from the bar and collected the bottles. "A lot has happened that doesn't make sense to me," he said thoughtfully. "Once I have Caroline across a table from me, *then* I'll know how to deal with her. It's simply a matter of where. Suppose you were in her place," he said slyly. "What would stop you driving a couple of miles to see me? Always remembering that she *wants* me, Mac." He had the feeling that Arran was insane. The thin, handsome face was troubled yet not unduly. As if Arran sought no more than reassurance. "She may well want you," Bain answered. "But she doesn't trust you. Maybe you're losing sight of the reason why we're making this trip. I'm bringing you home, remember? A bad boy." He leaned back, settling in the low seat, taking the heat of the sun on his face with gratitude. Eyes shut, he added : "She's still got to be sure that she has this weapon to threaten you with. Bring her to Spain and she loses it. She's no fool," he urged. "She knows well enough that a Spanish cop won't be interested in her squawks about us. And she knows you know it." He took the risk deliberately. Arran must still have a subconscious resistance to return to Gibraltar. If he recognised it, transferring the source of danger to Caroline, so much the better. As the motor hummed Bain opened his eyes.

Arran was putting on dark glasses. "I could have done a lot with you," he said. There was no smile on his face now. "Sometimes you show an insight I never suspected. You're right, of course. We can leave the car in the square, this side of the Spanish customs. Then walk across to the British control and take a taxi into Gibraltar. That way, there'll be no nonsense with *carnets*." He reached for his driving glove.

Slumped as he was on his shoulder blades, Bain fished the keys from his pocket. This could be his last opportunity. They swung from his forefinger, bright polished steel glinting in the sun. "Look!" he said and made a lazy arm to dangle the keys under Arran's nose. "Remember?"

Arran took the keys in his left hand as if fending a blow. He hefted their weight, thoughtfully. Neither man spoke. Watching Arran's expressionless face, Bain saw the North End Road—the long forbidding bulk of the squad cars. The cop's voice, coming across the pavement, still shocked his ears. "Since your friend Corrigan didn't want them, I kept them," he said steadily. "I always figured you'd tell me what to do with them."

Arran threw them with a sudden gesture of distaste. They landed on Bain's knees. Squinting, Bain saw the ridged prints on barrels and wards. "And the gun?" asked Arran.

"Twenty feet under water," answered Bain. He made no move to touch the keys in his lap. "I had no further need for it, after the other night." He turned the switch of the radio idly—as if neither time nor place had importance.

Arran's fingers reached out, gripping Bain's hand, twisting it free of the control. His voice was venomous. "You bloody fool! Sooner or later, your play-acting's going to finish you. Get rid of them, *now!*" He jerked his head at the dark trees. "Or do you *want* to spend the next few years in jail?" he demanded.

Unhurriedly, Bain lifted the keys by the ring that held them. He thumbed the catch on the heavy door, swinging it open. He climbed out and stood there for a moment, bitter with the desire to answer yet afraid of the chance word that would provoke suspicion. Then he walked a hundred yards into the woods. Once hidden from the road, he crouched in the bush, packing the keys in the tin with utmost care. Wrapping it in a handkerchief, he stuffed it into his inside coat pocket. When he had rubbed his hand in the dirt at his feet, he ran for the highway, using the trees as cover. Forty feet from the car, he stopped. Motionless, he looked at the parked Jaguar. Arran sat casually but his hand was busy behind him, foraging Bain's bag.

Bain ran back a few yards and made a noisy exit. By the time he reached the car, Arran was gloved and roaring the motor with impatience.

"Not just dumped," Bain said. "But stuffed inches into the earth."

Arran nodded but covertly he inspected Bain's dirt-covered fingers. "Well, let's get going," he said. "And we'll be in time for lunch at the Rock. My wife appreciates good food," he said with composure. "Never underestimate the effect of good food on an irascible woman."

Bain made no answer. As the Jaguar whined down the long hill, he sank still lower in his seat, the outline of the cigarette tin hard against his ribs. Sweat streaked the dust on Arran's forehead. He slowed for the police at the junction to La Linea. A grey-clad cop swung an idle hand and Arran turned the Jaguar south. Here, the highway skirted the bay. Fishing boats bobbed in the blue shallows. Beyond them, travel-worn freighters, paint blistered red under the Mediterranean sun.

The road dipped, curving to a straggle of narrow streets, shuttered and empty. The only signs of life came from the square on the left. Straight ahead, two arches spanned the highway. The Spanish Customs police huddled underneath, checking the Gibraltar traffic. Arran turned the car into the square and parked in front of a café. Over by the deserted station, a bus creaked out in the direction of the Customs post. Back wheels splayed under its excessive weight. Steam leaked from the radiator. The passengers hung from open windows, indifferent to the discomfort. There was one cab with a sign on its windshield LIBRE. The driver was asleep at the wheel.

Arran threw the door open. He ran a comb through his hair. "You'd better take your bag with you, hadn't you?"

184

Bain climbed from the car. The heat from the pavement struck through his thin leather soles. He shook his head. "I don't see any point in it. I'll come back with you and take a bus into Algeciras. Then get the Spanish ferry to Tangier."

Arran kicked a shoeshine boy from under his feet. "Then we'll walk." He took Bain's elbow, almost as if he feared that the other might run.

Once under the arch at the Customs post, they had a half mile to walk to the passport control and the British side. It was a straight, bare concrete highway, edged with rusting wire. They kept to the narrow pavement, making slow time in the noonday sun. Haze blurred the outline of the great rock in front of them. Once, Arran stopped dead. Bain swallowed, his tongue dry with sudden fear. Grunting a little, Arran bent, easing his shoe. As they reached the frontier post, a bus was lumbering through the raised barrier. A group of four Spanish sentries sat in the shadow of their blockhouse, nursing their rifles. Only yards away, on the British side, a kilted Highlander stamped his beat.

Bain tapped on a window marked PASAPORTES. As the glass frame slid back, Arran was close at his shoulder. A clock on the wall inside showed ten minutes to one.

"Señor Ellis?"

Bain nodded, taking his passport under Arran's thin smile. His hands were trembling. He thrust them deep in his pockets, leaning against the wall. In a few seconds, they would be in British territory. Through the glass at the other end of the office, he could see a Gibraltar policeman, helmet tipped back, yawning. It all seemed too quiet. Too decently British and safe. The clock on the other side of the wall was ticking loudly. He could hear Arran's voice, courteous in Spanish, as he retrieved his passport.

Arran was first into the alleyway that led to the British control. Fifteen yards of paved walk, hedged with latticed wire. As the two men reached the far end, a buzzer sounded in the Customs building beyond. A door slammed and hatless, shabby, Inspector Farrell came towards them at a lumbering trot. Behind him were a dozen police and Immigration officials.

Arran wheeled swiftly. He was no more than inches from British soil. Using all his weight, Bain drove both hands at the other's chest. Arran clutched the wire, hanging as Bain fell. His mouth was opened wide and working as if he were shouting. But no words came. Then, vaulting Bain's sprawled body, he sprinted for the Spanish side. As he passed the window in the passport control, it flew open.

Bain forced himself to his feet, blood seeping from forehead and hands. All around him was a confusion of shouting voices. He pumped his legs in pursuit, his breath a strangling agony. Arran was thirty yards in front and gaining. Splay-legged with haste, Bain tripped on the edge of the pavement, falling once more. The Spanish passport official leaned from his window, his voice shrill with excitement. "Shoot!" he commanded. His arm pointed at Arran's back.

One of the soldiers knelt, sighting the running man. A warning shot cracked, echoing in the wooded heights of the rock. Arran was fifty yards away, now. Running in the middle of the concrete strip, his maimed arm flapping awkwardly. With the shot, he wheeled and made for the barbed-wire, the waste land, the water beyond. The official called from the window again. There was no compromise in his voice. The soldier took careful aim. At the second report, Arran stretched his arms in front of him and ran a few steps, tip-toed. Then he pitched on his face, kicked a small cloud of dust and was still.

"Olé!" called a second soldier with admiration. His dark face stiff with pride, the marksman got to his feet. Lagging a little behind him, as if in tribute, the three soldiers followed him towards the dead man.

The cigarette tin with its keys had spilled from Bain's

pocket. He picked it up and dusted the surface with care. At the end of the alleyway between Spanish and British sides, a group of police was crowding the exit. Drab in his civilian clothing, Inspector Farrell stood apart and behind.

Clutching the cigarette tin tightly, Bain limped towards the barrier and the man who was waiting for him.

THESE ARE PAN BOOKS

Nicholas Blake
THE WHISPER IN THE GLOOM
Action-packed mystery of murder and international intrigue in the London underworld. 'Thriller fiction at its best.'—*Birmingham Mail*.   (2/6)

Auguste Le Breton
THE LAW OF THE STREETS
Violent story of the men and women of the backstreets of Paris—where the gun and the razor are the only passports to survival. Tough and convincing.   (2/6)

Malcolm Gair
SAPPHIRES ON WEDNESDAY
Hard-hitting private eye is hired to steal a sapphire necklace. It leads him half-way across the world—with danger lurking around every corner. 'Full marks.'—*Daily Telegraph*   (2/6)

Francis Clifford
OVERDUE
Intensely dramatic story of a plane crash in the Arizona desert—with a murderer loose among the terrified survivors. 'Horribly exciting.'—*Spectator*.   (2/6)

PICK OF THE PAPERBACKS

www.ingramcontent.com/pod-product-compliance
Ingram Content Group UK Ltd.
Pitfield, Milton Keynes, MK11 3LW, UK
UKHW022313280225
455674UK00004B/292

9 781471 905636